“How are yo

girls?” I ask

“We’ll have t keep them right where they are. I’ve asked the deputies and ambulance to come into camp the back way, without sirens. Could you go back to the amphitheater and when the program’s finished get them involved in singing or something to keep them busy till we can talk to them?”

“Please don’t take too long or parents will start worrying.”

“We’ll do our best to move things along.”

When I returned to the group, the last of the emergency personnel was completing his critique, demonstrating the fine points of creating a makeshift tourniquet. When he finished, Latoya began to award certificates and badges which I knew would take at least a half hour.

Almost an hour later I almost missed the fact that Latoya was dismissing the girls. Only the roar of laughter that accompanied her final words aroused me from my thoughts, I was so mired in grief. I jumped to my feet to get everyone’s attention.

“Hold on a minute,” I yelled. “We have a problem on the other side of camp, and we can’t let you leave just yet. Let’s get Barb Kellerman to lead us in some camp songs.”

Barb had dealt with so many emergencies over the years she didn’t miss a beat but immediately rose to her feet with a smile and asked for suggestions.

As the group began to sing, Latoya came over to sit beside me. “What’s going on?” she whispered. I found a scrap of paper in my pocket, took the pen from Latoya’s clipboard and wrote “Evan McCandless is dead.”

★

Previously published Worldwide Mystery titles by
NANCY GOTTER GATES

WHEN PUSH COMES TO DEATH
DEATH AT PLAY

DEATH ON DISASTER DAY

NANCY GOTTER GATES

WORLDWIDE®

TORONTO • NEW YORK • LONDON
AMSTERDAM • PARIS • SYDNEY • HAMBURG
STOCKHOLM • ATHENS • TOKYO • MILAN
MADRID • WARSAW • BUDAPEST • AUCKLAND

For Dorothy, Librarian Extraordinaire.

DEATH ON DISASTER DAY

A Worldwide Mystery/September 2011

First published by Alabaster Book Publishers

ISBN-13: 978-0-373-26768-2

Printed in U.S.A.

Acknowledgments

The members of the Mystery Group I section of the Writers Group of the Triad are my sounding board as well as very dear friends. Their thoughtful critiques of my manuscripts are invaluable.

Many thanks to current and former members Diane Lambright Berry, Elizabeth DiMeo, Helen Goodman, Dorothy P. O'Neill, Wendy Greene and Ellen Elizabeth Hunter. And thanks to Tarheel Triad Girl Scout Council Executive Director Marci Brown for her input and suggestions.

ONE

I'VE ALWAYS CONSIDERED myself a brave woman—with one exception. I can't stand the sight of blood. I've been known to keel over while having a blood sample taken at the doctor's office. So when I walked into the large rectangular tent at Camp Galimore that May morning, it took every bit of determination I could muster not to turn around on the spot and leave. Just inside the front flap, sprawled in a director's chair, a middle-aged man wore a blood-soaked shirt, the result of a long, deep gash on his forearm. Beyond him a young woman sat in a lawn chair with her right leg propped on a camp stool, a wound running from her knee half-way down her leg. And there were at least a dozen others inside the tent whose bodies bore evidence of violent trauma.

I kept reminding myself that it was makeup and fake rubber wounds that I saw, thanks to the skill of makeup artists from the community theater. But the musty smell of canvas mixed with the odor of ether used to affix the fake wounds only increased the queasiness in my stomach. How I regretted that I'd given in to Evan McCandless when he'd asked me to be a "victim" for this exercise.

He'd called me a couple of weeks earlier at Stewardship Life where I worked.

"TOMMI POAG, GIRL. How are you?" his cheerful voice boomed over the phone. He'd handled my divorce from Bernard more than a year and a half earlier, and a friendship had developed between us. It was such a traumatic time in my life—Bernard had left me for a much younger woman in his law firm—and Evan struck just the right note between sympathy and tough-mindedness that helped me get through that terrible time with at least a modicum of equanimity. He and his wife Chris no longer played a large role in my life as I saw them only on occasion. But I knew he would be there for me should I need his help in any way.

"Did you know I was on the Girl Scout Board now?" he continued.

"No, you're kidding." I was delighted. I'd spent many years volunteering with the Girl Scouts even though I was unable to have children of my own. Bernard would never hear of adoption, so I "adopted" Brownies as a troop leader. Now that I was forced to go to work to support myself, I no longer had the time for it and I missed the pleasure it had brought me.

I knew that Evan would be a great asset for their Board. "And you don't even have a daughter to coerce you. Amazing," I said.

"Some of the female staff weren't too bad at coercion," he said, laughing. Though Evan liked to pretend he was quite the ladies' man, I felt that he and Chris were deeply in love. "But I didn't call to discuss my charming ways," he continued. "Remember Disaster Day?"

"I was never involved. My girls were too young." Disaster Day was an annual event which tested the older girls' first aid skills in a major exercise. It was held each spring at Camp Galimore about fifteen miles outside of Greensboro, North Carolina, where I live.

"Girls from all thirteen counties are participating this year so it's going to be a big one, and I'm playing victim. Wondered if I could talk you into it, too. They're having trouble getting enough volunteers."

"When is it?" I was praying I was busy that day. Having ketchup dribbled on me to represent blood was not my idea of a rollicking good time. I once observed it but stayed as far back from the scene as possible. Thankfully the ketchup had looked only like ketchup.

"May 12."

"Hmm." Even though I'd usually jump at any excuse not to clean house on Saturdays, I'd rather scrub toilets than be around disasters, real or fake.

"Come on, Tommi, we really need you. You know you don't want to let down all those girls who have worked so hard to earn their patch."

He sounded serious now. Evan could be the great persuader. He didn't get to be a top lawyer on charm alone.

"Well, I suppose..." I guessed I could deal with ketchup this one time.

"Cheer up, it will be fun."

"If you say so."

THE VOLUNTEERS WERE invited to a potluck dinner at the Bur-Mil Park clubhouse the night before the exercise to get our instructions. I had been eating TV dinners for so long I hardly remembered how to cook but finally made a vegetable dish that had sour cream and almonds with enough fat and cholesterol to send my doctor into shock. I was one of the last to arrive and when I entered the building I saw Evan and Chris in the far corner waving to get my attention. I added my casserole to the dozens on the serving table and joined them, especially pleased to see that Ty and Melanie Tyler and Latoya Griffin were at the table, too. Melanie had been a Brownie leader for years, and we had attended many meetings together. Latoya was a Field Director, a member of the paid staff. Otherwise, I didn't see many familiar faces.

Latoya got up and hugged me. She'd always been my favorite of the staff members, young, slender, attractive with her black hair smoothed back into a bun and glowing mocha-colored skin. It was her somewhat irreverent attitude that I most admired. Latoya loved her job, but she had no illusions about herself or her importance. As she'd said many times, it was the volunteers who contributed most to their success, without them there would be no Girl Scouts.

After hugs all around, the six of us filed through the food line and returned to the table, plates brimming over. The heady combination of enticing odors and noisy chatter made me nostalgic for the "good old days," times that would never return. Not that my life with Bernard had been all contentment. He'd never been an easy man to live with. But I'd had the leisure time for occasions like this.

Anyway, I was glad to have this opportunity to see Evan and Chris. I watched them across the table, totally absorbed in each other. Evan was not handsome in the traditional sense. His features were too uneven, with a nose that slanted to the right and a large mouth fixed in a perpetual grin that revealed uneven teeth. He was the kind of man who invited mothering.

Chris, in contrast, never had a hair out of place. Even today, dressed in a yellow T-shirt and brightly flowered skirt, her hair in a stylish short cut with subtle highlights running through it, she was the polished sophisticate.

The Tylers were quite a different pair. Ty Tyler was a handsome man with thick black hair cut neatly to conform to police department standards where he was a patrolman. He had piercing blue eyes and a trim little mustache. Melanie was a sweet woman and enthusiastic volunteer. She was short and stout, her weight problem exacerbated by having three children in four years. I was very fond of Melanie but thought she was one of the plainest women I'd ever known. I credited Ty with unusual maturity for choosing character over superficial beauty.

I had just cleaned my plate when Evan got up, walked around the table and leaned over my shoulder. "I know you want second helpings, don't you? I do, too."

He pulled back my chair then took my arm and guided me toward the serving table.

"Now what's the real reason for dragging me over here?" I asked, sensing it had nothing to do with food.

"I thought you'd be interested in knowing I'm suing your ex for malpractice."

"Bernard! Over what?"

"It's kind of involved. Several years ago my client was injured in a car accident. She felt her doctor bungled her treatment so she went to Bernard. He told her she didn't have a case, and he failed to suggest she could consult someone else."

He stopped for a minute to take a piece of cake.

"Then the statute of limitations ran out for suing the doctor," he continued, "and she learned she had a viable case after all. Now she's suing Bernard for bad advice, and if she wins that one she can sue the doctor."

"Poor old Bernard," I said, mostly tongue in cheek. "He must be furious."

"Let's just say I'm not one of his favorite people."

I laughed. "So what else is new? He knows what you could have done to him in my divorce suit, that you begged me to let you. But, of course, I was too proud. There are days when I'm sorry I didn't let you go ahead, the days when I look at my bank account. False pride can be really stupid."

I thought back to those terrible days when Bernard told me he'd fallen in love with a much younger lawyer in his firm. I just wanted to get through it, to get OUT. My mind was so fuzzy it was impossible to think straight. What else could Evan have done? It was my fault I got such a pitiful settlement.

"I tried to tell you, Tommi," Evan said, putting his arm around my shoulder and giving me a hug.

"I know."

"Well, anyway, I thought you ought to know about the suit, that maybe it would give you a little satisfaction."

"I'd like to say I'm past that stage." I paused, then I laughed. "But I wouldn't mind seeing him squirm."

TWO

As I stood reluctantly in the doorway of the tent the next morning wishing I could think of some excuse to leave, someone tapped me on the shoulder. I turned to see Latoya grinning at me, no doubt aware of my hesitation.

"Pretty grisly, isn't it?" Latoya was in charge of the day's exercise. The Field Directors took turns each year planning the annual event, and this was Latoya's first time to take over. She'd explained the night before that she intended to make it the most realistic one ever. She'd even found a junkyard owner who agreed to have two smashed-up buses towed to the camp property and arranged to look as if they'd collided. I longed for the old days when everything about the exercise was fake. "I figure if the kids can handle this," Latoya gestured around the tent, "they'll be able to deal with the real thing some day."

"Right. If they don't faint or throw up, they'll do just dandy," I replied, wondering which one I might do.

"These kids have seen so much mayhem on their video games and at the movies, it won't even faze them."

"You've got a point," I acknowledged.

The "victims" were scheduled to be made up in two shifts and I was in the second batch. As I circled the tent looking for my makeup artist, I came upon Melanie Tyler. A woman swathed in a stained smock was painting fake abrasions on her cheek, and she had what appeared to be a black and swollen eye.

"Having fun?" I asked her.

"I don't know if fun is the right word," she replied, staring into a mirror. "It's too real for my taste. But I suppose it's too late to back out now." She clutched the arms of the chair so tightly her fingers had gone white.

"Do what I used to do at scary movies. Keep your eyes shut," I advised her.

I came upon Evan at the back of the tent.

"I'm glad Chris isn't here to see you," I told him. His fake head wound looked particularly awful. It was a great open gash just below his hairline with lots of fake blood running down the side of his face. He was covered with a sheet to protect his clothes.

Suddenly he thrust out his arm and I let out a yelp. It looked as though he had a compound fracture with a jagged bone protruding grotesquely from his lower arm. My stomach gave a lurch.

"That's horrible," I protested.

"I thought you'd like that." Evan put his arm back under the sheet and laughed like a kid. "What wonderfully gory things are going to happen to you?"

"I don't know, but I'd better find Peggy Isaacs to see what she has in store for me"

I found her in a far corner of the tent just finishing up on another volunteer.

I sat on the folding metal chair as soon as he left. "Am I going to have any bones sticking out?" I asked.

"I think we've run out of bones," Peggy answered. "How about a sprained ankle and a facial laceration?"

"You're the boss."

I closed my eyes and let her do her thing. Thirty minutes later I heard someone say "Wanna look?" I opened my eyes and Peggy was offering me a mirror. An ugly gash began near my temple and crossed my cheek diagonally down to my chin.

"Oh, my, I'll be scarred for life." Of course, I was kidding, but I could almost believe it was true. She'd done a masterful job.

"The doctor says a little soap and water will do wonders for you."

Peggy then used blue, green and purple paint to make my ankle look bruised. I began to think I could feel pulsing pains in my ankle and foot. The power of suggestion.

"Yo, victims!" Latoya stood at the door of the tent, raising her voice over the din. "It's about time to arrange the bodies down by the buses. Are y'all ready?"

"Ready!" everyone shouted in unison. What a sight they were. Limping and moaning, with some self-conscious giggling breaking out now and then, the group followed Latoya down a well-worn path to the clearing in the woods where the buses had been arranged head-to-head in a simulated crash.

Gathered in small clusters around the perimeter of the clearing were a half-dozen sheriff's deputies and emergency personnel who'd volunteered to help. They were readying medical supplies and stretchers.

Latoya took the "injured" and placed us carefully inside and outside of the buses, like a living tableau of horror. She led me inside the worst looking bus where we had to brush aside stringy cobwebs as we went down the aisle. Layers of dirt and rust had coated everything making it difficult to see out the filthy windows. "Wait till I give that Evan a piece of my mind," I muttered under my breath. "He's at least going to have to take me out to lunch to make up for this."

Latoya pointed to the aisle floor near the rear. "Why don't you lie down here, as if you've been thrown from a seat."

I gingerly let myself down onto the grimy floor, protecting my left ankle as if it really hurt.

"We're not giving out Oscars today," Latoya teased. "You can relax."

"Not me," I said. "Not till this thing is over."

Latoya just chuckled. She brought four more volunteers into the bus and placed some of them draped over seats, some sprawled against windows. As she left the bus for the last time she said, "Now don't move. I'll be back with the kids shortly."

"Hurry," I prayed. "Let's get this over with."

THREE

It was unnaturally quiet as we waited for the girls to arrive. The odor of mildew and decay was almost overpowering on the bus, and I heartily wished I could have been outside.

At last I could hear the muted voices of the girls as they came down the path from the administration cabin where they'd been kept out of sight until everything was ready for them. The voices grew louder as they approached the clearing when suddenly there was complete silence. I was sure that the gory scene had struck them dumb. They never would have suspected that the exercise would be so close to reality. Then, filling the void of sound, low moans began, growing louder as the volunteers felt less foolish. The cacophony increased as they realized they could indulge their theatrical fantasies to the limit.

Within a few minutes a handful of Scouts

climbed aboard the bus and spread out in groups of twos or threes to help the injured. Two teenagers dressed in old jeans, T-shirts and anoraks approached me.

They treated me with gentleness, although I could tell they were somewhat daunted by the scope of the exercise. Little nervous gestures gave them away, but they cared for me with the seriousness and skill they would have given a real victim. I was impressed with these girls.

"We can't get a stretcher on the bus," the dark-haired girl said when they were finished. "We're going to make a seat with our arms to carry you out."

They helped me stand up, and I clung to a bus seat, holding the leg they had splinted in front of me. When they locked their arms together, I lowered myself onto this human chair and put my arms around their necks as the girls edged slowly down the aisle of the bus. When we got to the staging area, two men helped me off their arms and eased me down onto a stretcher on the ground while the girls explained to the emergency personnel what they had found in the way of injuries and how they treated me.

Finally, all the injured were treated and brought

to the area where I waited, relaxed now on my stretcher. Latoya signaled for quiet and spoke to the group. "Now that we're finished with this part of the exercise, we're going to the amphitheater for a critique. The volunteer medical personnel are going to tell you what you did right and what didn't go so well. Listen to them carefully because this is going to be very helpful to you. Then we'll give out the First Aid certificates and badges."

The girls let out a unanimous cheer as the tension of the exercise dissipated in the May air. They hurried en masse down the path toward the large outdoor seating area which consisted of two rows of giant logs planed flat on one side and laid in a large double ring.

As they left, the "victims" rose up from the stretchers or camp seats, unwinding bandages, taking off splints and pulling off fake wounds in an eerie spectacle that resembled a massive faith healing.

Soon everyone was seated in the amphitheater, girls on one side, adult volunteers on the other. Latoya stood in the center directing the critique. I began looking around the ring to see how my friends had fared. Melanie was sitting on the front row listening intently. I searched the ring for Evan, but I couldn't find him. I checked each row carefully again, thinking I had overlooked him or he'd been temporarily obscured by someone else. But this time I was sure he was not there. What was he doing, playing hooky? I'd have to give him a hard time over that, the rascal.

Since I had no part in this critique, I decided to sneak off, too. I wanted a chance to enjoy the solitude of the woods. Camp Galimore was very special to me, and I always felt a sense of renewal when I strolled its paths. The dogwood was past blooming, and it was too early for the rhododendron, but the trees had leafed out, filtering the sunlight in the dense woods.

I slipped out as unobtrusively as possible and made my way back toward the clearing which seemed strangely tranquil after all the frenetic activity. Only the trampled undergrowth indicated a crowd had been there. In the hush of the forest a wood thrush trilled up and down the scale as though rejoicing that this place belonged to him once again.

I continued along a narrow path that led to Possum Creek which meandered along the northern edge of the camp property. I sat on the bank, slipped off one shoe and sock, and stuck my toes in the icy water. If that didn't wake me up, nothing could. It would be some weeks yet before it was wading time.

As I dried off my foot, I noticed something blue under a tree on the far side of the creek, farther down toward the edge of camp property. Had someone thrown trash there again? Because the creek was so close to the property line at that spot, too many people dumped their old mattresses and assorted cast-off household goods down its bank instead of taking it to the city dump where they had to pay a fee.

I put my shoe back on, crossed the creek on flat rocks that jutted out of the water and hurried along the far bank, cursing under my breath at the disgusting habits of the jerks who had done this.

Several yards away, I stopped in my tracks, horrified. The blue thing was a shirt on a limp human body, the legs stretched up the bank away from the creek, the face submerged in water that was only a few inches deep. No amount of fake blood or fake wounds had prepared me for this. My head felt light, my face flushed and a wave of violent nausea doubled me over. I had to get the head out of the water, but my whole body rebelled at the thought of touching it. Surely he must be dead, it appeared to be a man, but it would be obscene to leave his face submerged that way. Or maybe he had just slipped and hit his head and was still alive. I didn't really believe that, but I couldn't take the chance.

Gathering every ounce of self-control and praying for the strength not to run away, I knelt down, grabbed a hank of hair and pulled the head out of the water, half rolling the body on its side. Oh, my God, it was Evan! I didn't realize I had screamed until I heard the faint echo from the woods. The blood from the dark red hole in his forehead had mixed with the fake blood creating a crimson stain in the little pool of stagnant water encircled by a giant oak tree root.

Stunned, I sank to a sitting position, staring at him. I could not accept the reality of what I saw. I had seen so many fake wounds that day; was my mind playing tricks on me? A shudder went through me. No, this was all too real.

I felt incapable of functioning; it was if my body and mind were hung up in neutral, but I knew I had to tell someone as soon as possible. I remembered there were sheriff's deputies at the amphitheater. I'd go get one quietly…I didn't want the girls to see this. How could this ever have happened?

FOUR

I STARTED BACK toward the amphitheater, my legs working as if they belonged to somebody else. A cloud shrouded the sun for a moment, casting a shadow over the clearing that had been gloriously bright not fifteen minutes earlier. The wood thrush was no longer singing, and an eerie silence enveloped the woods. The two battered buses were slouched on the ground like the decaying remains of dead mastodons.

I began to run, slowing my pace when I came out of the woods so as not to attract attention. I spotted one of the deputies sitting on the back row, his back to me. I walked over to him and whispered in his ear.

"I've got an emergency. Could you come with me, please?"

He looked up at me with a question in his eyes, and I put my finger to my lips for silence and pointed toward the woods. He got up quietly and followed me till we were out of sight and hearing of the others.

"What's up?" he asked. He was a solid, muscular man in his late twenties or early thirties. His boyish face framed by dark hair belied his muscular body.

"Something terrible's happened." I almost couldn't get the words out my mouth it was so dry. "One of the volunteers is dead."

The deputy reached out and grasped my shoulder gently. "Ma'am, I know this thing was awfully real seemin'. I think you got caught up in all the emotion of it."

He must have thought I'd gone round the bend.

"I'm not imagining it," I said, trying not to let my impatience show. "Let me take you there." I pulled away and hurried down the path through the clearing and over to the creek, checking to make sure he was following me. I led him along the bank to the tree where Evan's body lay sprawled, his face now turned toward the sky, his staring eyes fixed on the heavens as if looking straight into the Beyond.

The deputy stooped down, felt Evan's neck for a pulse, shook his head and closed the staring eyes with gentleness. He got up and put his arm around my shoulder, this time in sympathy. "Do you know him?"

"It's Evan McCandless." My voice caught as I said his name. "He was my divorce lawyer. He's on the Girl Scout Board, and he asked me to be in this exercise. You can see that he was made up to be a victim."

"I don't remember seeing him."

"I know. I spoke to him in the tent during the makeup session, but I don't recall seeing him after that."

"I'll call it in on my cell phone." He pulled it out of a holster on his belt and called the Sheriff's department.

After he hung up I asked him, "How are you going to handle this without involving the girls?"

"We'll have to ask them some questions. But I want to keep them right where they are. I've asked the deputies and ambulance to come into camp the back way, without sirens. Could you go back to the amphitheater and when the program's finished get them involved in singing or something to keep them busy till we can talk to them?"

"Please don't take too long or parents will start worrying."

"We'll do our best to move things along."

When I returned to the group, the last of the emergency personnel was completing his critique, demonstrating the fine points of creating a makeshift tourniquet. When he finished, Latoya began to award certificates and badges which I knew would take at least a half hour.

Almost an hour later I almost missed the fact that Latoya was dismissing the girls. Only the roar of laughter that accompanied her final words aroused me from my thoughts, I was so mired in grief. I jumped to my feet to get everyone's attention.

"Hold on a minute," I yelled. "We have a problem on the other side of camp, and we can't let you leave just yet." The sheriff would have to announce Evan's death. I couldn't form the words without breaking down. "Let's get Barb Kellerman to lead us in some camp songs."

Barb had dealt with so many emergencies over the years she didn't miss a beat but immediately rose to her feet with a smile and asked for suggestions.

As the group began to sing, Latoya came over to sit beside me. "What's going on?" she whispered. I found a scrap of paper in my pocket, took the pen from Latoya's clipboard and wrote "Evan McCandless is dead."

The field director looked at me in shocked disbelief and started to rise from her seat, but I grabbed the back of her T-shirt and pulled her back down. Then holding my hand so low no one else could see it, I formed a gun the way a child does with thumb and forefinger. Latoya could only shake her head in deep sorrow.

I thought I could not endure sitting there listening to the jaunty camp ditties while Evan's body was being examined only a few hundred yards away. The girls joined in enthusiastically at first but began to get restless as the singing continued on and on. Finally, when I was afraid the girls would start wandering away, three men came out of the woods and entered the circle. One was the deputy I had directed to Evan's body, but I did not recognize the other two, one in uniform and one in blue jeans. The singers stopped abruptly, and a hush hung over the group as they realized something abnormal was happening, something ominous.

The man in the blue jeans introduced himself. "I'm Sheriff Barger." He looked more like an accountant than a law enforcement officer with his wire-framed glasses and precisely trimmed gray hair. "I have some very sad news to announce to you," he said. "One of the volunteers who was participating in this program has been killed."

"Who?" cried one of the women volunteers, her voice shrill with alarm.

"Evan McCandless, a member of your Board of Directors," he replied. There were exclamations of "Oh, no!" and "Oh, my God!" around the circle as most people there at least knew of him. Someone cried out, "What happened?"

"He was shot. We don't know the circumstances yet, but there is a good possibility that someone hunting or target shooting could have done it accidentally and was not even aware of it." He pulled a handkerchief out of his pocket, took off his glasses and wiped his face. "We don't want to keep you here any longer than necessary, but we do need to interview everyone at least briefly. Deputies Kronenberger and Davies and I will divide up the group between us."

With Latoya's help to organize the interrogations, each man interviewed one person at a time. The sheriff asked to speak to me first. I described how I found Evan and that I'd turned his body in pulling his head out of the water. I was afraid they'd be upset that I'd touched him, but they seemed to understand that I had to make sure that he wasn't still alive. Otherwise, I'd neither seen nor heard anything unusual until I stumbled upon his body. I repeated that I'd last seen Evan alive in the make-up tent.

After my interview, I saw Melanie hunched over on the other side of the amphitheater crying softly while the woman beside her offered her a discarded sling to wipe her tears. I went over to console her, although I badly needed consoling myself.

When I sat down beside her, my presence triggered a new onslaught of tears. Her words came out garbled.

Finally, she made herself understood, hiccuping as she spoke. "And…to think he was near me…out there. If only he didn't have…to go to the bathroom."

"What?" I asked. "You saw him during the exercise?"

"Sure," she said wiping her eyes again. "He was probably ten or fifteen feet away from me. He told me he was desperate to go the bathroom, but he wanted to make sure that none of the girls could see him. I'm sure he was embarrassed to ask me about it, but you know how careful you have to be nowadays about things like that. I told him the camp boundary was just beyond the creek."

"Come on," I said getting to my feet and taking Melanie's arm to help her up. "You need to tell this to the sheriff."

"I was just trying to get composed first," she murmured. She followed me over to the sheriff who was interviewing one of the girls.

When he finished, I stepped forward. "I think Melanie has something that might help you," I said.

Melanie repeated what she'd told me.

"And he never came back?" he asked.

"No, sir," she said. "I didn't think much about it. I assumed either he'd gone somewhere else or he decided to leave camp altogether. By then the exercise had begun, and I frankly forgot about him."

The sheriff took her name, address and phone number and said he might want to talk to her again.

"Could I go home now?" she asked. "This has torn me all to pieces."

"Yes, go ahead. And thanks for the information."

Tears started to flow again, and Melanie, still clutching the sling, used it to wipe her eyes.

"Are you all right to drive?" I asked. "I'll be glad to take you home."

"Thanks, hon, but I'll be okay. Ty should get off work pretty soon."

I walked her to her car and saw her off and then returned to the amphitheater.

IT WAS ANOTHER HOUR before everyone was questioned. As the sheriff and deputies prepared to return to the death scene, I asked Latoya, "Don't you think it would be better for us to tell Chris rather than have the sheriff do it? I'd hate to hear the news from a stranger."

Latoya grimaced. "You're absolutely right, Tommi, we should. But it's the last thing on earth I want to do."

"You couldn't possibly dread it more than I do. But maybe with the two of us we can get through it."

FIVE

FORTUNATELY TRAFFIC WAS light on the way to Evan's house from camp as I found it next to impossible to keep my mind on my driving. I kept wondering what I was going to say to Chris, and in fact, whether I could tell her without breaking down.

The McCandless house was an impressive Georgian-style mansion in Irving Park surrounded by a bent-grass lawn that seemed an extension of the golf course behind it. I pulled into the drive behind Chris's BMW. As I unbuckled my seat belt, I could tell by the look on Latoya's face that she was feeling apprehensive, too.

Chris greeted us with pleasure and surprise when she answered the door. As always she looked bandbox neat though she wore faded jeans and a sweatshirt with Evan's alma mater "Duke" in bold letters. She was holding a bottle of window cleaner and had a roll of paper towels under her arm, but her makeup was impeccable and her hair stylishly protected by a folded bandanna tied behind her head.

"Tommi! Latoya! How did the exercise go? Did Evan behave himself?" She laughed, apparently at the thought of the mischief he might have wrought as the indefatigable cutup.

My stomach churned at Chris's cheerfulness.

"Come in and have a seat," she continued. "Can I get you coffee or a Coke?" She preceded us into the room chatting amicably about the exercise.

Latoya and I followed her, but we didn't sit down. Instead I reached out and gently grasped my friend's free hand. Chris looked at me in puzzlement, her smile fading now, and she put down the bottle and roll of towels on an end table.

"What is it, Tommi? Is something wrong?"

I could barely make my voice work. "I think you'd better sit down."

Chris's face drained of color as she sank slowly onto the rose-and-cream-striped damask couch. She said nothing, waiting for me to continue, but her expression told us she already had a good idea what I was going to say.

"There was a terrible accident..." I struggled to keep going. "Evan was shot out at camp."

"Shot? What do you mean shot? I thought you were going to say he was in a car accident or something. How could he get shot at a Girl Scout camp? Where is he?" Chris's voice hovered on the edge of hysteria.

I realized that she still did not understand. "Chris," I said as gently as possible, "Evan is dead."

"Dead!" She let go now, succumbing completely to her emotions for probably one of the few times in her life. "I don't believe it. How could it be?" Her eyes were fierce, ready to do battle with anyone who insisted on this absurdity.

Latoya sat down beside her and spoke gently, trying to calm her. "We're not sure what happened. The sheriff's out there now investigating."

"They think it was either a hunter or someone target shooting outside camp property," I said. "Apparently they are unaware of what they've done."

Chris covered her face with her hands, and her body shook with sobs. By the time she lowered her hands, her face was covered with little rivulets of mascara that looked like bruises on her cheeks.

"Where was everybody else?" she demanded. "Was anyone else hurt?"

"He was out of sight of the others. He'd gone

over to a nearby field to relieve himself according to Melanie Tyler."

"Oh, no. Oh, Evan." It was a wail of agonizing sorrow.

Latoya laid her hand on Chris's clasped hands. "There must be something we can do to help."

Chris just closed her eyes and rocked silently back and forth. After a while she said, "Where did they take him? I want to see him."

"The sheriff said he would call you as soon as they had taken him to the hospital. Can we stay here with you until he calls?" I asked.

"Oh, please," Chris replied.

I finally sat down in one of the elegant side chairs next to the couch and an awkward silence filled the room. Chris seemed to be totally preoccupied with her thoughts, and Latoya and I occasionally exchanged imploring glances, hoping the other would know the appropriate thing to do or say. But inspiration did not come. I thought about the last time I'd been in this house. It had been a New Year's Eve party, and we had played silly word games. With his usual inventiveness, Evan had made up hilarious definitions for arcane words that had the group in tears from laughter. Whenever Evan joined a group, it seemed a bit more spirited than without him. I knew his death would leave all of us with a void impossible to fill.

Just then the phone rang. It was the sheriff saying that Evan's body was at Cone Hospital if Chris wanted to come view it. If an autopsy was needed, it had to be done in Raleigh, some eighty miles away.

We drove there in my Honda, Chris slumped in the front seat in a disconsolate heap. I knew she would never have gone out in public dressed the way she was under normal circumstances, but she seemed totally unaware of that now. She had not even repaired her makeup but simply wiped her cheeks with the back of her hands which only smeared the mascara more. We drove in silence.

The receptionist at the front desk of the emergency room was expecting us and directed us toward a far corner of the treatment room, where Evan's body was being kept behind discreetly drawn curtains. A Dr. Helmsburger guided Chris into the cubicle where she stayed for only a brief time. When she emerged, she was sobbing again and her hands were shaking. Latoya and I helped her to a chair in the waiting room, and a nurse's aide brought her a drink of water.

"It can't be true. It can't be true," she repeated as if it were a mantra.

We took her home, stayed with her while she notified relatives, fixed her a light meal which she ate under protest and finally left when she thanked us profusely for our help but told us she needed some time alone.

SIX

I WAS PLAGUED with terrible dreams that night. I was directing the Disaster Day exercise, but to my horror the volunteer "victims" kept turning up dead, dying from the fake wounds that had been applied by the makeup artists. When I woke at 2:30 a.m., my sheets damp with sweat and clinging to me in spite of the coolness of the air, I was too unnerved to go back to sleep. Instead I did my ironing that had been piling up for a couple of weeks. There was something about the back and forth motion that helped soothe me; it had the mesmerizing effect of waves lapping rhythmically on the shore.

By morning I was exhausted, but I couldn't take the chance of going back to bed and another round of dreams. Instead I shuffled around in my housecoat and slippers like an eighty-year-old, which was exactly how I felt. Even my cat, Tee, seemed to sense that something was wrong. He hid under the couch instead of tripping me up as usual while I fixed breakfast.

I didn't open the newspaper until I'd finished eating my Honey Bunches of Oats and toast, and had stacked my dishes in the dishwasher. Normally a leisurely reading of it was part of the Sunday breakfast ritual, but I knew Evan's death would be front-page news, and I didn't want to see it in black and white. That would make it a fact, and for the past twenty-four hours I'd tried my damnedest to deny that reality.

Finally, I settled into my Bentwood rocker and reluctantly unfolded the *News and Record.* Evan's picture was in the top right-hand section of the front page, and a lengthy article covered just about every point I already knew. I was dismayed but not surprised that my name was mentioned as the one who found the body.

Sheriff Barger was quoted as saying that although the investigation was continuing, all evidence pointed to accidental death. He urged anyone with information about persons hunting or target shooting in the area to contact his office, emphasizing that if the person responsible turned himself in, the D.A. would file only minimum charges. But his benevolence would be short-lived. If those responsible knowingly kept quiet, the D.A. would "throw the book at them" if their involvement came to light later.

I wondered if this not-so-subtle threat would have any results. How would I react in such a situation? Even the most law-abiding citizen would be totally unnerved if he thought he might have accidentally killed someone. Isn't that what often happened in hit-and-run accidents? Panicky people do some very unnatural things.

The shrill ring of the phone on the table beside me caused Tee to bolt from my lap.

"It's Bernard," my former husband said when I answered it. As if I wouldn't always recognize his voice, no matter how long we had been apart.

"Hi," I said dully, wishing I'd let it ring. I had no desire to talk to him now. For the first months after our divorce our paths rarely crossed. Then we were thrown together for a while in a case involving his cousin. Now we occasionally saw one another on social occasions, but nothing short of a miracle could eliminate the tension between us. And I have never believed in miracles.

"I wanted to tell you that I'm sorry about Evan."

"I appreciate that." Was he really all that sorry?

"Do you honestly think it was an accident?" he asked me.

"What kind of question is that?"

"I know you liked him, Tommi, but quite frankly he had you snowed."

"Look, Bernard, I can understand that you personally weren't fond of him. Your animosity was quite evident during our divorce, and I'm sure you know that he wanted to do a lot more damage, but I chickened out." I'd never mentioned that before, but if he was going to defame Evan's memory, then I had no compunction about reminding him that he was the guilty party and was lucky to have gotten off as easily as he did.

"He had a very inflated notion of his abilities."

"Oh, yes, that's right. I heard he'd filed a malpractice suit against you." I wished I could see his facial expression right now.

"That was purely malicious. He had nothing to go on. That's what I'm trying to tell you. It's far from the first frivolous suit he'd filed. To put it bluntly, Tommi, he was about as popular as the plague with a number of people."

He was acting like a pouty little boy. The man was dead for heaven's sake; why didn't Bernard grow up and forget it? "Well, don't get carried away.

The sheriff feels sure it was an accident. Do you think you might have an overactive imagination?"

"Just a passing thought. Pamela says to tell you hello."

"Ditto to Pamela," I replied, applying my thumb to my nose and wiggling my fingers. When I caught my reflection in the mirror on the wall, I blushed. Who was the childish one now?

After I hung up, I thought about our conversation. I knew Bernard disliked Evan, but I hadn't realized how much. Of course, who would like his ex-wife's divorce lawyer? And the malpractice suit seemed to have clinched it. But surely he couldn't be right about so many other people disliking him. That was the first time I'd ever heard about it.

SEVEN

LOGAN STAHL CALLED later that evening. Logan was my boss, an agent for Stewardship Life. The two of us ran the small office located on the second floor of the fifty-year-old Piedmont Building on Eugene Street. He sold life insurance policies, annuities and an occasional small group health policy while I serviced the policies, typed, filed and did the computer work. It was a great no-stress, low-key, fairly interesting job, though I did occasionally get bogged down in boredom when there wasn't enough to keep me busy. The main problem was it didn't pay very well. But then I had no job history so what could I expect? Not much. I felt lucky to have it.

I sometimes wondered what my life would have been like if I hadn't dropped out of law school to marry Bernard and had pursued a career of my own. From what I learned being a lawyer's wife, I'd decided that while there might have been some prestige and, for sure, much more money, it was basically a very boring profession. Unless you're in trial work or in criminal law, it mostly amounts to stacks and stacks of paperwork. But the worst part is the stress and long hours. No, I probably would have burned out early on.

"I just got back from the mountains," Logan said. "What a shock to see your name on the front page. Wasn't he your lawyer?"

"He was. And a terrific guy, too. I still can't believe it."

"Why don't you take all of tomorrow off. I see the service is at two. No sense in coming in at all."

"Thanks, Logan."

I was grateful for the time off, but I didn't want to be alone. I decided to go to the Girl Scout office the next morning out on West Market Street and commiserate with Latoya and the rest of the staff.

When I arrived at ten, the atmosphere at council headquarters was funereal. Instead of the usual lively banter, the main topic of discussion was Evan's death. Most of the staff knew him fairly well, probably better than they did other Board members since he'd overseen the cookie sale. Usually a paid staff member would have been in charge, but the Finance Director moved out of town unexpectedly when her husband was transferred, and Evan had volunteered to fill in until a new Finance Director could be hired. He'd talked about it the other night at dinner, regaling me with stories of the girls' sales prowess and how some had sold hundreds of boxes. He was as proud of them as if they'd been his own daughters.

Barb Kellerman, the camp director, and Latoya were in the small upstairs room they shared.

"Hey," said Latoya as I entered their room. "What're you doing here?"

"My boss gave me the day off. And I couldn't bear the thought of sitting around home by myself."

"Sit," Barb commanded, pointing toward a small wooden chair in the corner. "Maybe you can help us figure out how to turn things around."

"Meaning what?"

"I was telling Latoya that our camping program is probably down the tube. I'm already getting calls from parents who want to cancel their kid's reservation. I'm afraid it's going to snowball, and nobody will come."

"Oh, brother," said Latoya. "That's such a big part of our program."

"The worst part is we could lose serious money,"

Barb said. "I have fixed expenses whether there's any income or not. This could wreck our budget."

"Couldn't you write the parents and reassure them it's safe out there, that it was a freak accident?" I asked.

"You're kidding, of course. Would you be reassured?" Barb was twirling the ends of her frosted curly hair around her finger.

"No," I admitted. I picked up a rubber band from Barb's desk and began to fashion a cat's cradle.

"I can't figure it," Latoya mused. "There are 'no hunting' and 'no trespassing' signs all over the woods."

"Well, some idiot obviously ignored all the signs," Barb said. "Unless they find this guy and put him away for a while, we're in deep trouble."

"Even if they find him, parents are going to worry about somebody else doing it," Latoya said. "Short of putting up a six-foot barbed-wire fence with armed guards outside the camp boundary, they'll be sure it can happen again." Latoya always offered the worst-case scenario for everything.

"You are aware, aren't you, that the sheriff says the D.A. will go easy on the person if he turns himself in," I said.

"'Minimum charges.' That probably means no

jail time." My rubber band broke suddenly and flipped into Barb's lap.

Barb snatched it by one end and held it up. "Then here's what's going to be left of our camping program," she said. "Zip…zero…zilch."

They closed down the Scout office that afternoon so that the entire staff could attend Evan's funeral at Forbis and Dick Funeral Home. The whole front of the chapel was engulfed in towering banks of flowers. It certainly didn't appear that he was friendless as Bernard claimed.

After the service, I joined the procession to Forest Lawn cemetery though Latoya and Barb returned to the office with the rest of the staff. The graveside service was brief, but I, one of the last to arrive, couldn't get near Chris because of the crush of friends conveying their condolences once more. I decided that it hardly mattered if I spoke to her now. With this crowd, Chris would never remember who talked to her. She would need me far more later, after things got back to "normal." That meant normal for everyone else but not for the bereaved. I still remembered vividly how friends consoled me at the time of my divorce, but it wasn't long before many of them drifted away, oblivious to my loneliness and pain.

As I drove home, I was unable to get my mind off Chris. What did she have left to her, anyway? She had nothing but that great big house and its fancy furnishings. I wondered if loneliness wouldn't be magnified with so much space to be lonely in. I vowed I would see Chris often as soon as her parents had left and she'd handled the most urgent of the paperwork that always faces the survivors.

On Tuesday I returned to work but my spirits didn't improve much. Logan was out of the office most of the day calling on clients, and I had stacks of filing to do, the part of my job that I loathed. All my other duties were okay, but filing was like dusting: endless.

It was nearly quitting time when Chris called me. "Tommi, I've got to see you. Can you come over?" Her voice wavered unnaturally.

"Of course. What is it? You sound so upset."

"I'll explain when I see you."

"I'll come straight over. It'll take about twenty minutes."

By leaving a little before five, I beat the rush hour traffic which was getting progressively worse in Greensboro, a town of nearly two hundred and fifty thousand.

The cloying scent of flowers was noticeable as

soon as I stepped into Chris's house. Every table top, the mantel and the piano were covered with elaborate flower arrangements. I didn't like it; it was too much like a funeral parlor.

Chris was alone. She looked pale and sad and was fidgety, twisting her wedding ring around and around on her finger. She explained that her parents had left that morning at her insistence. "They have their own lives to lead, Tommi. They couldn't sit around holding my hand for weeks. I've got to learn to make it on my own. What I called you about was an insurance investigator who came to see me a little while ago. I thought since you worked in insurance, you could tell me what to do."

"An investigator? Whatever for?"

"Evan took out a $750,000 policy about nine months ago. He'd once mentioned something about getting more insurance, but to tell you the truth, I never asked about the details, and he never told me. He always handled the business end of things, and I guess it never occurred to either of us that I ought to know more about it."

I nodded my head knowingly. I, too, found out the hard way I should have been more involved in things like insurance and taxes during my marriage.

"I know it's pretty inexcusable. Maybe working women pay more attention to these things. But Evan handled most of it at the office, and I never even saw the paperwork."

"So what's this about a guy from the insurance company?"

"It seems he's here because the policy has been in force less than two years and has a double indemnity clause."

"So it's just a routine investigation. It's standard under these circumstances. Nothing to get alarmed about."

Chris shook her head and looked worried. "I'm not so sure. He had about as much charm as a rattlesnake. He kept asking me what I was doing Saturday morning. When I told him I was home cleaning house, he asked if I could substantiate that."

"Could you?"

"No. I never saw anyone from the time Evan left till you and Latoya came."

"And he wouldn't take your word for that?"

"He seemed very skeptical. He wondered why I didn't have maid service to clean such a big house. When I told him I'd never found anyone who satisfied me, and I preferred to do it myself, he looked at me like I was lying through my teeth."

"Well, I can vouch for you. Let's face it, you're

one of the few people I know who actually likes to clean house." I'd hoped to bring a smile to Chris's face, but my efforts fell flat. "What can I do to help?"

"Talk to him. I'm sure he'll want to interview you, anyway, since you're the one who found Evan. And knowing something about the insurance business, perhaps you can set him straight about me or at least find out what's going on."

"Of course I will. The man's grasping at straws." I didn't have the heart to tell Chris that I'd never had a death claim investigated since I'd been with Stewardship Life, and I knew very little about it.

EIGHT

Before I could get in touch with the insurance investigator, he contacted me. I'd barely had time to stick a frozen dinner in the microwave when he called and arranged to come to my house that evening. I had mixed feelings about talking to him. I resented the way he'd grilled Chris. Even though it was his job to ask questions, from the sound of it he had done it with very little tact or compassion. To put her through such a painful experience the day after the funeral was inexcusable. On the other hand, I was curious about what he was looking for. Had something led him to believe Evan's death was not accidental? It was ridiculous to suspect Chris. But I couldn't help thinking about Bernard's phone call. Was there any merit in his assertion that Evan had enemies?

The doorbell rang on the dot of 7:30 p.m., our appointment time, and I hurried to open the door.

Tee fled to the bedroom to seek safety under the bed as he always did when strangers came.

Carter Raines smiled with the self-confidence of a handsome man as he introduced himself and produced identification showing he was an investigator for Midlothian Life Insurance Company. He was more than six feet tall, apparently in his early forties and had the artificial good looks of a model, and the air of a man who knew he attracted attention. I could see the flash of red suspenders beneath his navy suit coat, and he was self-confident enough to sport a bold tie in outsize paisley interlaced with a floral design. A less intrepid man would have been embarrassed by its gaudiness.

He perched stiffly on the edge of my antique Hitchcock chair instead of choosing the more comfortable sofa. I sat, as usual, in my rocker. He opened the fancy leather briefcase he carried and glanced quickly through a sheaf of papers several inches thick. The rustle of paper sounded unnaturally loud in the stillness that hung between us. This little period of silence was no doubt meant to intimidate. I wished I'd turned on the radio to an easy listening station. Better yet an acid rock station. That would have shaken his imperious self-confidence a little.

At last he laid the papers on the table beside him and looked at me with his intense blue eyes.

"I understand you were the one to find Mr. McCandless's body."

"I'm afraid so."

"Can you tell me in detail everything you did and saw?"

I wondered how many times I was going to have to tell this dreadful story over and over. I was beginning to feel a kind of detachment by now, a distancing I sensed was vital to keep from falling apart each time someone asked me about it.

Raines took copious notes as I talked, occasionally interrupting me to clarify a point or to ask for more detail.

"And then you and Miss..." He grabbed up the papers to search for the name.

"Griffin."

"Oh, yes, Latoya Griffin. You went to the McCandless house to tell Mrs. McCandless about her husband?"

"Yes."

"Did she seem genuinely surprised by the news?"

I couldn't believe this joker. "Of course."

"Do you feel certain that she had no prior knowledge of his death? Was her shock and grief absolutely convincing to you?" He stared at me levelly, not in the least uncomfortable about asking such a question. What a cold son-of-a-gun this guy was.

"Look, I knew them well. Evan was my divorce lawyer and we've been good friends. They were a very happy couple, and I cannot even conceive of Chris doing what you are implying."

"But you don't know for sure what she was doing while you and Evan were involved in the exercise. Is that right?"

"I have every reason to take her word that she was cleaning house. She is absolutely fanatical about cleanliness, and she does it all herself because no one else can do it to suit her."

"But there's no proof she was involved in housework at that time."

"No….but I also can't believe she's such a good actress that she could have faked her reaction when we told her. The woman was devastated. I'm sure she wasn't putting it on."

"You'd be surprised at what good actors people can be when a lot of money is involved," Raines said as he rapidly wrote in his notebook.

I decided that he'd been born cynical.

"Oh, no," I replied, shaking my head slowly. "You're wrong about her. Don't you take the sheriff's word for it that it was probably a hunter or someone target shooting?"

"No one's come forward, and they have no suspects. That's not good enough for the insurance company. Not when a big policy had recently been purchased. Particularly one with double indemnity, it's imperative to look at the beneficiary."

"She told me he bought it without her knowledge."

Raines gave me a look of withering skepticism without saying a word.

"That's all you have to go on?" I asked. "Just the fact she can't prove where she was at the time? That's pretty slim isn't it?"

"I've also heard he may have been having an affair. A wife who wants revenge can be mighty tempted to do him in if she can wreak her vengeance and collect a tidy sum at the same time." He started to smile a knowing smile and then apparently thought better of it and arranged his features into a serious, businesslike mask.

"Where on earth did you hear that?"

"His secretary, Annalee Turner."

I was surprised he was telling me this so readily. But if I closed my eyes and listened to him talk without being swayed by his good looks, he sounded like the village busybody who got off on spreading petty gossip. It seemed unprofessional. Then it occurred to me that it might be a very canny way of getting me to open up and say things I wouldn't ordinarily reveal. I couldn't decide whether Raines was a loose cannon or an extraordinarily crafty investigator. So I said nothing but simply stared back at him.

"Well, have you heard any such rumors?" he asked.

"Absolutely not."

He shook his head and wrote some more in his infernal notebook.

"I hope you aren't planning to say anything about this to Chris. She's suffered so much already." I suspected my plea was falling on deaf ears. "Have you found out anything else? Has anyone else come under suspicion?"

"I've just begun. No telling what might turn up."

I stood. I'd had enough of Raines. "Well, I guess that is that."

He placed his materials back in his briefcase with deliberation while I waited impatiently for him to leave.

"I hope you'll let me know if you find out anything new," he said.

"I hope you'll do the same for me," I replied. "I'm anxious to see this thing settled not only for Chris's sake, and I know you'll find she's innocent, but for the sake of the Girl Scouts. Their camping program has been destroyed, and I don't think it can be salvaged until they find the real perpetrator."

"Don't worry," he said. "We'll find the perp all right, but you might not like the outcome." His eyes, brimming with self-importance, held mine for a minute, and then he was gone.

NINE

THE NEXT EVENING I sat at the counter that divided living room from kitchen and picked at an unappetizing TV dinner. I scooped out portions of the so-called chicken potpie and spread it out on my plate trying to determine its contents. It seemed to contain a lot of potato chunks, a few small carrots and infinitesimal pieces of what may have been chicken floating in globules of "gravy." I wished I knew a gourmet cook who hated to eat alone. It was my bad luck that my single friends were no more inclined to fix a decent dinner than I was.

I always turned on the TV when I came in, more to dispel the silence that permeated the house during my absence than to watch a particular show. I hadn't realized that the local news was on till I heard the word "murder." I swivelled on my stool to see what it was about.

Chet Newsome, the anchor, was speaking. "A New York-based insurance investigator, Carter Raines, with Midlothian Life Insurance Company, was found shot to death behind a building on Davie Street this morning."

I felt as if I'd been struck by a bolt of lightning.

Newsome continued. "Mr. Raines was here to investigate the death of prominent local attorney Evan McCandless. At this time the police see no apparent connection between the cases. It is believed the motive was robbery, but there are no suspects at this time."

I could not believe it. People were dying all around me. This didn't have the impact Evan's death had on me, I had intensely disliked Raines, but I was shaken by this alarming turn of events.

I sat in front of the TV set through the rest of the news, staring at the screen, hoping that more information might be released, but it never was.

I dialed Chris's number as soon as the news was over.

"Did you hear about Carter Raines?" I asked when Chris answered.

"Tommi? Is that you? What are you talking about?"

"It was just on TV. Carter was shot to death. They found him in an alley downtown."

"You've got to be kidding! Who did it? What happened?"

"They say it was an apparent robbery. They haven't arrested anyone, though."

Chris was silent for a moment. "You don't suppose I'm off the hook now, do you?"

"What do you mean?"

"I suppose the insurance company will send another investigator who'll start insinuating awful things about me, too."

I didn't know what to say. "Well, yes, I suppose they'll send someone else. I would hope he wouldn't act the way Carter did."

"Will it never end?" Chris sounded so disheartened that I was worried about her. "I want to figure out how to get on with my life. That's all. If they'd only leave me alone."

"I'm sorry," I said. "I wish there was something I could do to make it better."

"You've done everything you can. Particularly the way you straightened things out with Mr. Raines."

I felt a surge of guilt at that statement. I'd reported back to Chris about Raines's visit, but I'd whitewashed it as much as possible, insinuating that he'd decided to pursue other directions. Technically it was true, since he mentioned the possibility of an affair, but he'd certainly not dismissed her as a possible suspect. Chris evidently thought I was responsible for redirecting him, and I had not known how to set her straight without mentioning Raines's allegations. I'd put myself into a corner, so I accepted Chris's gratitude rather than hurt her further.

After I hung up, I tried to read, but I couldn't concentrate. Finally, I gave up and stared without comprehension at some sitcom rerun.

Shortly after nine the phone rang, much to my relief. I wanted desperately to talk with somebody, anybody, who could get my mind off Carter and Evan.

"Oh, Tommi." The voice sounded strangled and I couldn't make out who it was.

"Who is this?"

There was a minute or two when all I could hear were snuffling sounds and heavy breathing, and I began to wonder if it was an obscene phone call. Finally, in a stronger voice, the person spoke. "It's me, Pamela." Bernard's new wife.

Pamela! I hadn't talked to her since the divorce

proceedings, and I hadn't planned on ever speaking to her again, God willing. I could not imagine why she would call.

"Well, yes…hello."

Silence.

"Is something wrong?"

I heard a stifled sob. "It's…it's Bernard."

Good God, was Bernard dead, too? I was to the point where if someone said the world was coming to an end, I would have believed them.

Pamela finally managed to continue. "They've arrested him. For Evan's murder."

I was speechless. It was absurd! I finally found my voice again. "What are you talking about, Pamela? Everybody knows Bernard would never do such a thing. It's preposterous."

"Not to the police. They took him to headquarters just a little while ago. He wouldn't let me go along."

"Tell me what happened. From the beginning."

"Please, Tommi, come over here. I've got to talk to you."

The woman I loathed most in the world was begging for my help, and for a moment I was incapable of reacting. Of course I felt sorry for Pamela, who was obviously devastated, but the idea of going to her home, the one she shared with Bernard, was so repugnant that I was paralyzed by indecision.

"I don't know..." was all I could manage to say.

"I understand how you feel." She was silent for a moment, and when she spoke again her voice wavered. "I don't blame you if you hate my guts."

How perceptive, I thought testily. My resentment didn't disappear just because Pamela wanted to kiss and make up now that she needed me.

"But can't we call a truce for now?" Pamela continued. "Would it help if I came to your house instead?"

Pamela was beseeching me, her voice so plaintive she sounded like a condemned prisoner begging for her life. I knew I had nursed this resentment much too long, that my bitterness toward Pamela did far more damage to me than it ever hurt her. I knew all this in my mind, but my heart was still having trouble with it. It was time, though, to act like an adult and find out what the woman wanted. Furthermore, at this point I was extremely curious as to why they had arrested Bernard.

"No, I'll come there," I said. "I doubt you're in any shape to drive."

The house that Bernard and Pamela owned was in one of the newest developments that bordered

Lake Jeannette. Instead of the Georgian houses like Evan's which had always dominated the most affluent neighborhoods, these ran the gamut of styles. The Poag house was faced with diagonal boards of natural wood with a curved towerlike structure on the front that contained a spiraling staircase seen through strategically placed windows, as well as small odd-shaped windows scattered randomly across the facade. Instead of a peaked roof, it slanted downward from left to right, and the front door contained a Mondrian-like design in stained glass. It was not only an astonishing departure from the traditional architecture of Greensboro, but was the direct opposite of what Bernard had chosen to live in with me. I long ago decided that this was another statement to the world that he was starting over—a new wife, and a new and totally different house. The only thing he was unable to change was himself. He was still the rigid, pompous workaholic that he'd always been.

When I rang the doorbell, Pamela answered almost immediately.

"Please come in," she said, waving me into the foyer. Pamela was what I thought of as more handsome than beautiful. She had dark hair cut in a neat short pageboy, and large brown eyes that looked so steadily into your eyes when she spoke, you felt compelled to break eye contact first. Her features were not at all dainty, but rather sharply defined so that there was a touch of masculinity in her appearance. Not enough to detract, but just enough to give her a look of competence and authority. What few times I had been around Pamela, I had always felt a little intimidated by her.

That was why it was so surprising to see her now, her eyes red and puffed from crying. She had on shorts and a T-shirt, quite a change from the severe navy or black suit that I had always seen her wear. So the stalwart Pamela had a vulnerable side. It was an unexpected revelation that gave my feelings about Pamela another little shove toward empathy.

I followed her through the foyer toward the back of the house. We entered an enormous great room that was furnished sparsely with a sectional sofa, two uncomfortable-looking chairs made of leather slung on metal frames and some wrought-iron-and-glass tables. The colors were drab and the few accessories were scattered on mantle and tables like an afterthought. The furnishings were too small for the scale of the room and looked lost in all that space.

The room itself was quite lovely with a glass wall

across the back and a huge stone fireplace made of flat rocks dry stacked in a seemingly helter-skelter fashion. It was truly a masterpiece, but its impact was lost in the drabness of the decorating. I felt guilty pleasure to discover that Pamela did not excel in all things.

We sat on the sofa which had seats too deep for comfort.

"I can't tell you how much I appreciate your coming," Pamela began.

I nodded without comment.

"I can't believe this is happening. It's too bizarre."

Pamela dug for a hankie in her pocket and blew her nose.

"Tell me from the beginning," I prompted her.

"There was a sheriff's car parked in front of the house yesterday when we got home from work," she began. "Normally we both work late, but we were invited to a friend's house for dinner so we left right at five so we could come home and change.

"Sheriff Barger asked to come in to talk to us. There was a deputy with him. We both assumed they were going to question us about Evan. You know, how long had we known him, and so on. Just to get some background information. Instead he asked if we would give consent to a search of the premises to check out an anonymous tip. He said it was no doubt a crank call so they hadn't gotten a warrant, but they figured Bernard would understand their need to go through the motions, anyway. Bernard asked what it pertained to, and they told him someone had seen him out near the camp on Saturday around the time of Evan's death."

"And what was Bernard's reaction?"

"He told them he was working at his office at that time. He thought some lawyer with a twisted sense of humor was trying to pull a monstrous joke on him. He told the sheriff it was ridiculous but to go ahead as long as they didn't make a mess. They were very apologetic about it."

"Why didn't he make them get a warrant?"

"We knew we had nothing to hide, and it would just drag the whole embarrassing thing out. We just wanted to get it over and done with." Pamela paused for a moment and wiped her eyes. "Forty-five minutes later they came back with a rifle. They said they found it behind the woodpile in the garage. We'd never seen it before and told them so, but they took it in for tests."

"And it checked out."

Pamela nodded forlornly. "I couldn't believe it.

They came an hour ago, read him his rights and took him away. Bernard has never owned a rifle as far as I know. I'm sure you're aware that hunting never interested him in the slightest."

"He used to have a .22 which he kept in the nightstand for protection," I told her. Although he hadn't done criminal law in decades, his stint with the Public Defenders' office many years ago had made him a little paranoid.

"That's right," Pamela said. "He still has it. I forgot about it. I wonder why the sheriff didn't take that, too. They must have seen it when they went through the bedroom."

"Are you sure it's still there?" I asked.

"Of course. I'll get it and show you."

While Pamela was gone, I got up to inspect the fireplace. It was the only thing in the house that I coveted though it would take up the entire living room of my condo.

Pamela returned to the room half running. "It's not there, Tommi. I looked all around the bedroom and it's gone."

"You're positive the police didn't take it?"

"They would have said something."

"Do you think it might be at his office?"

"No, someone has taken it."

I found that hard to believe. Bernard probably moved it without Pamela's knowledge. "Who and why would someone do that?"

"I haven't a clue. I have a regular cleaning lady, and repairmen have been here now and then. Who knows?" Pamela sank back down onto the couch with her elbows on her knees and supported her head with her hands as though bereft of the strength to hold it up another minute. Finally, she looked up at me. "The reason I asked you to come tonight is I need your help."

"Help you? How?"

"Bernard will ask someone from our firm to represent him. I'm just sure of it, he's so loyal to them. But none of them are criminal lawyers. I'm afraid they'll make a hash of it."

"What's that got to do with me?"

"You know him better than anyone outside of myself. And you knew Evan well. Couldn't you do a little digging and find out who might have wanted Evan dead? The sheriff isn't going to bother. They're sure they've got their man. But you and I know they're wrong. And remember, Tommi, you were able to prove the police wrong when Cap Sellars was killed."

I nodded. "Bernard may be a lot of things, but he's definitely not homicidal."

"So can't you come up with some other suspects? Did you meet that insurance investigator, Carter Raines? When he talked to us, he brought up some questionable things about Evan, like rumors he was having an affair. And he seemed to have some doubts about his wife's alibi, too."

"You know that Raines is dead, don't you?"

"What!" Pamela's hand jerked to her mouth.

"I guess you were too busy to watch the evening news." I noted that Pamela either missed or ignored the irony of my statement. "He was found shot to death downtown this morning. They think it was a robbery, but they don't have any suspects."

"This is getting weirder by the minute, Tommi. There's got to be a connection here."

"It would seem so. But I guess it's possible that it could be a coincidence."

"No way!"

I was startled by Pamela's outburst. She'd always been so in control, at least around me. Maybe she was human after all.

She spoke quietly but with great urgency now. "Please help us. You may not realize it, but it's just as difficult for me to ask this of you as it is for you to agree."

I felt pulled in many directions. But Pamela's plea was so heartfelt it was almost impossible to turn her down.

"Okay, I'll do what I can. But don't expect too much."

TEN

THE NEXT MORNING'S paper had a quarter of a page devoted to Bernard's arrest. I was sitting on the sofa, still in my pajamas and robe, trying to read it, and Tee kept trying to wiggle under my arms to get to my lap. I finally gave in to him knowing I'd have no peace otherwise. Holding the paper high to make room for him, I read all the details which Pam had been unable to tell me the night before. The reporter made much of the fact that both men were prominent attorneys. He quoted the sheriff as saying the malpractice suit Evan had brought against Bernard could well have been a motive. And the article suggested that there had been bad blood between them since our divorce case. He quoted a secretary in Bernard's firm who described how the men had scuffled in the hallway outside of the conference room after a settlement negotiation.

I remembered the incident vividly. Evan had let

himself become emotionally involved in the case as a friendship developed between us, and he'd been disappointed by my refusal to "take Bernard to the cleaners." After a frustrating session, Evan had called Bernard "a cheap shyster," and Bernard had retaliated by shoving him so hard that Evan slipped and fell. It was only because other lawyers restrained them that they didn't come to blows. I was mortified that this episode was now a part of the public record.

According to the article, Bernard became a suspect when the sheriff received an anonymous tip placing him near Camp Galimore the morning Evan was killed. The tipster also reported hearing Bernard make threats against Evan. Bernard make threats? I couldn't imagine it. When Bernard got mad, he tended to quit speaking and would sulk for hours. I'd sometimes long for a screaming match; it would have been so much more satisfying. I never knew how to deal with his silence.

The rifle they found in Bernard's garage had the registration number filed off and had been wiped clean of prints. And, of course, it had been used to kill Evan.

There were pictures of both men. Bernard's had been taken when we were still married and he'd been elected president of the local bar association. Bernard looked quite solemn and dignified as he thought befitted the office. Evan's picture seemed more recent. It showed Evan's boyish grin and tousled hair and contrasted dramatically with Bernard's staid pose. Those pictures said so much about each of them, it broke my heart.

I was glad that Logan was in the office when I arrived at work. He planned to make his sales calls later in the day.

"I can't believe what I read in the paper this morning," he said. His normally cheerful expression had been replaced by an unusually solemn one. "It's going from bad to worse rapidly. The whole thing is unreal."

"Anything I can do?"

"Can I have a few days off? I've got lots of vacation saved up." Lack of both money and a traveling companion made trips a rare occurrence. "I told Pamela I'd try to help them out."

"Your nemesis?"

"The very one."

"Are you sure this is something you want to do?"

"She's kind of pitiful right now. I've always been intimidated by her, but she's really not as self-assured as I'd thought. Maybe if I could help in getting them out of this mess, it might exorcize some of my own demons. At least I'd not feel like 'poor little Tommi' the abandoned wife anymore. It would be an ego trip to have her in my debt. And, of course, I want to know who really did it. Bernard may be a lot of things, but he's not a murderer."

"Since you put it that way, go get 'em. Take all the time you need," Logan said, laughing.

"One more thing. Do you know anybody at Midlothian? I'd love to know what Carter Raines found out about Evan. It might have something to do with Carter's death."

"You don't think it was a robbery?"

"I believe in coincidence up to a point. But don't you think it's a little much to take that at face value?"

"Well, I admit I sure had some doubts about it, too. Anyway, I know Hank Wasserman who's been with Midlothian for years. I'll check with him and see if he can find out anything."

"Thanks, Logan. I'll check in with you now and then."

As I left, I wondered how to proceed. Truthfully, I wasn't at all sure I could even make a dent in this case. But I'd promised Pamela, and I knew in my heart Bernard was innocent. What about the telephone call he made to me? Would a killer admit how much he hated the victim? Not without calling a lot of attention to himself. And he certainly wouldn't tell his ex-wife who still felt resentment over his infidelity. Not if he had any sense, he wouldn't. And Bernard was anything but foolish.

THE FIRST THING I needed to do was talk to Bernard. Since he probably had limited visitation rights, I called Pamela and asked her to make the arrangements. Within a few minutes Pamela called back saying it was taken care of, and I could go at any time.

As soon as I was dressed, I drove to the county jail which was on Eugene Street.

I was directed to the visitors' room by a stern-looking female deputy. It was a small beige cinder block room with one wall filled with what looked like tellers' windows in a run-down bank. The only difference was there was no pass through to the other side. There were five windows separated by perpendicular wooden dividers with a small shelf running from corner to corner. By each window was a phone receiver to talk to the prisoner on the other side. There was nothing to sit on. Since the visitations were limited to fifteen minutes, the authorities apparently saw no need for a luxury like a chair.

I was already stationed before a window when Bernard was brought in. I was shocked by his appearance. He's a tall, slender man whose thick head of dark hair gives no hint of gray. The only change time has made is in the increased definition of the widow's peak by the hair receding on either side. He has deep brown eyes under heavy eyebrows and a long, straight aristocratic nose. Since he is not prone to laughter, he has few lines on his face, a face that rarely betrays any emotion. Normally cool and unruffled, today he appeared more vulnerable than I had ever seen him. Instead of standing ramrod straight, he was slightly stooped with his whole body conveying a sense of weariness, a loss of hope. The fluorescent orange prison jumpsuit that he wore seemed ludicrous on a man who normally wore expensively tailored suits and silk ties. And he already had the shadow of a beard that said more about his state of mind than anything else.

He stood opposite me and picked up the phone that connected us. "I'm surprised to see you here," was his greeting.

"I guess I could say the same about you." I couldn't resist.

"Touché."

"Aren't they going to let you make bail?"

"It's very high. Pamela's getting the money together but it will take a little time."

I got right to the point. "I don't know if Pamela told you or not, but she's asked me to dig around and see what I can find out about Evan's death."

"She didn't tell me. She knew I'd be furious. Which I am."

"I might have known your pride would outweigh everything else."

"It's not pride, Tommi. You shouldn't get dragged into this."

"I didn't have to agree to it. But I'm here. Who's your lawyer?"

"Jack Tomacetti. From my firm."

Pamela was right. His loyalty to the firm outweighed common sense. "What does he know about criminal law?"

He looked at me for a moment without answering. Finally, he said, as if to defend himself, "He'll be hiring his own private investigator."

"Well, maybe I'd better bow out, then. Don't want to step on anyone's toes."

He studied me silently for a few minutes, rubbing

his jaw as he often did when confronted with some weighty problem. “Pamela called you, you say?”

“Last night. I went over to your house to talk to her.”

“I guess you realize how hard that was for her.”

“For her? Frankly I was more in tune with my own feelings at the time.”

“Well, it had to take an enormous amount of guts for her to contact you. It would be a slap in the face to tell her I asked you not to do it.”

“So what are you saying?”

“Go ahead if you want to—it can’t hurt. You have the advantage of knowing the people involved in this.”

“‘It can’t hurt’? What a ringing endorsement.”

“Do you want me to get down on my knees and beg you now?”

He was incorrigible. I should thank my lucky stars that I didn’t have to live with him anymore instead of feeling sorry for myself. “Right now I feel like telling you to take a flying leap, but I won’t. I’m going to spend some of my vacation time trying to save your neck, but I’m not sure why.”

Bernard looked hangdog now, an expression I’d never seen on his face before. “I’m sorry, Tommi.

That was inexcusable. But you have no idea what being here can do to you. I'm not myself."

The hell you're not, I thought. "The paper mentioned that an anonymous caller said they saw you out near camp the morning Evan was killed. Were you out that way?"

"No, I'd gone to the office to catch up on some work. Actually, I was working on my defense for the malpractice case. But no one else was there for once, so no one could confirm it. Isn't that ironic, though? It's the malpractice case that's supposed to be my motive."

"I know. I can't imagine anyone killing over something like that."

"People murder for a lot less."

"I guess you're right. I just don't like to admit it. Anyway, I'm going to talk to some people. In the meantime is there anything I can bring you? Something to read? A hacksaw?"

He was too unstrung to smile. "Thanks for coming, Tommi," he said tonelessly.

"Goodby, Bernard," I said and hung up. I started to leave but turned around and went back and picked up the phone again. Bernard, who had not yet moved, reached again for his receiver. "I believe in you," I said. "I'm sure that you'll get out of this okay."

He hung up his phone and lowered his head so I could no longer see his face.

ELEVEN

I DECIDED THAT the best place to begin was to talk to Annalee Turner, Evan's secretary, to find out what I could about his so-called affair. I telephoned the offices of Jeffress, Rigoliso and Latham and asked to speak to her.

Annalee agreed to see me at eleven. "I've pretty much got Evan's things squared away, and I'm really just marking time until they bring in someone else," she said.

I had dressed in my best Sunset Drive style, one I had substantially discarded since my divorce. I now wore casual, comfortable clothes in keeping with my current lifestyle. But I still had some of the simple but expensive dresses I used to wear. Today, anticipating that I would see Annalee, I thought it might be helpful to reassume temporarily the essence of my life as the wife of a highly successful lawyer. I didn't plan to intimidate her, but social standing might be useful at a time like this. I'd learned in the past year or so that it was all a crock, but maybe Annalee hadn't discovered that yet. Did I feel guilty resorting to snobbery? Not if it accomplished my goal, to get her to open up.

When I arrived at the law office, Annalee greeted me warmly, with a slight deference I noted with satisfaction, and asked if I would like to talk in Evan's office where we could have more privacy.

His office was the same as I remembered it, yet different. It was as staid as ever with its paneled walls and Queen Anne furniture which had always seemed such an unlikely setting for Evan. All of the personal items, the diplomas, the photographs, the desk accessories and most of the books were gone. So were the personal touches like the collection of outrageous and sometimes raunchy lawyer figurines that friends had given him, the high school sport trophies he'd kept all these years and several antique toy fire trucks. The room's character had vanished as though Evan, in his death, had drained it of very atom of his uniqueness and taken it with him.

There was a plump sofa covered in a flame-stitch pattern under the window, the only comfortable piece of furniture in the room, and the two of us sat at opposite ends of that.

Annalee was an attractive young woman, probably around thirty, with her blond hair twisted into a French knot. It would have looked old-fashioned, anachronistic on most, but the effect of the slightly flyaway fine blond hair around her face gave her a fresh Scandinavian appearance. Her eyes were a deep brown, and her complexion glowed as if she had begun to work on a tan already. It was rumored that she'd done some modeling at one time, and I was surprised she wasn't still doing it; she certainly had the look. I wondered more than once what Chris thought about her. With Evan's proclivity toward flirtation, it seemed to be begging for trouble to put two such attractive people in close proximity for hours every day. Still, I had always believed that Evan and Chris were unusually happy together and that his flirtatious ways were harmless, merely his way of making other people feel good about themselves.

"Annalee, I'm getting right to the point. The insurance investigator who was on Evan's case came to see me, and evidently he talked to you, too."

"Oh, you mean Mr. Raines. Wasn't that horrible

about him getting shot? It makes you wonder what's going on in the world."

"The police say it appears to have been a robbery."

"Yes, and they said at first Evan was killed by hunters, too." She paused and her face turned crimson. "Oh…ah…I'm sorry. That was thoughtless of me." She must have suddenly remembered my relationship to the "murderer."

"Don't apologize. What I wanted to ask you was about something you told Raines. He said you thought Evan was having an affair."

Annalee's complexion glowed even pinker. "That was supposed to be a private conversation. I didn't think he'd go spreading it around."

"He told me in hopes I would corroborate it and maybe come up with additional information. I'm sure he was playing people off one another on the theory that if we all figured something was already common knowledge, then it was all right to tell everything we knew, even if we were sworn to secrecy."

"Well, it still upsets me."

"At this point it isn't going to make much difference, is it? The only person it could hurt is Chris, and all she cares about is solving Evan's murder."

"What about the person he was involved with? Not that I actually know who it was."

"My lips would be sealed. Unless it had something to do with his death. Then, of course, I would have to make it known."

"I feel funny talking about this. It seems to me we shouldn't pry into his private life now that he's gone. Telling Raines was different. He was from out of town and didn't really know Evan."

I thought it was a heck of a time to become so righteous. "It's a little late now, isn't it?" I said. "If you told Raines, who knows how much he spread it around. Besides, Bernard's life is a lot more important than Evan's reputation at this point."

"Well..." She seemed chastened. "I can't tell you who it was. I just felt something was going on because of his behavior. For instance, the door between our rooms was always open unless he was in a conference. But occasionally, he'd close the door to make a telephone call. I thought it was sort of strange since I knew everything that was going on in regards to cases. There was no point in keeping any secrets from me. And he even left the door open when he talked to Chris."

"That's it?"

"After those conversations, he'd rush off sometimes but he wouldn't tell me where he was going. I think he was meeting her."

"That's not very concrete, Annalee. Is that all you know?"

I could tell Annalee was peeved at my skepticism. She smoothed back her hair and picked up a throw pillow and plumped it up while apparently deciding whether to say more. Finally, she put the pillow back down and looked at me with defiance. "I think it was someone connected with the Girl Scouts."

"Why do you say that?"

"Because this all started after he joined the Board of Directors. He sure seemed to like going to Girl Scout things."

I thought Annalee was overreaching on that supposition. Evan was the sort who threw himself into volunteering. Whatever he did, he did with enthusiasm and gusto; he was a cheerleader for good causes. I couldn't imagine that he'd found himself a mistress among the staff or volunteers. I knew them all.

If Evan had been fooling around with anyone, which I certainly hoped was not the case, I would have guessed it would have been Annalee. I wondered if all this could be a case of sour grapes on her part. Maybe she'd been attracted to Evan and he wouldn't give her a tumble, so to retaliate she decided to tarnish his reputation. Or maybe she had some kind of grudge against Chris and wanted to throw a monkey wrench into the insurance settlement. It was even possible that she indeed had something going with Evan and was trying to throw Raines off the track. Heaven knew what went through her mind.

"You don't have the slightest idea who it might be?" I asked again, trying not to sound skeptical. "Never heard a first name mentioned or what her job or position was?"

"No, he always closed the door. I really don't have any proof. It's just a gut feeling."

"I see."

I was sure I wasn't going to get any more information out of Annalee, but I decided to talk to Wesley Cheloff before I left the building. Wes had joined the firm about the time Evan had, and I thought there was something of a friendly rivalry between the two; at least Evan had spoken of it that way.

I asked Annalee to check to see if I could talk to Wes now. Annalee was glad to oblige, in fact she seemed quite cheerful now that I wasn't going to ask her any more questions.

Cheloff said he could give me a few minutes. Annalee directed me to his office which was two doors down the corridor. It had the same paneling, the same formal furniture, but Wes's was unrelieved by anything like Evan's statuettes or trophies. But then Wes was totally unlike Evan. Heavyset, and wearing thick dark-framed glasses, he was probably around Evan's age, 32, but he looked older. His hairline had edged up at either side of his forehead leaving a narrow band down the middle like some half-completed Mohawk cut. His belly, which had been ample when I met him two years ago, now strained at the buttons of the pink shirt and rolled over his belt. I had heard that he was brilliant, had the top grades in his law school class, but he did not have the personality or appearance to attract clients. I had realized, after talking with him only briefly when I first met him, that he had absolutely no sense of humor and a deep sense of inferiority.

"Hi, Wes, how's it going?" I said, trying to establish a friendly atmosphere. I had a hunch that he wasn't going to open up readily.

"Fair to middlin'," he said as he always did with a slight whine. I wondered again if the unpleasant quality of his voice came from a deviated septum or low self-esteem. I would have bet on the latter.

"I hate to bother you, Wes. I know how busy you must be." I loathed the obsequiousness in my voice, but I'd put myself into a fawning role I couldn't get out of without making my dislike of him obvious. "I wanted to ask you about Evan. Could you tell me anything about his relationships in the office? How you felt about him?"

"Sure, I'll tell you." He finally waved me to the chair that faced his desk. "I'm kinda glad to get it off my chest. I've kept my mouth shut for years, and that's probably why I've got ulcers. Did you know I have ulcers, and I'm only 30?"

Good, lord, he was even younger than I thought. He looked at least ten years older than that.

"I'm sorry to hear that, Wes." I furrowed my brows as if I were truly concerned about his health.

"Well, your friend Evan is responsible for that. The Golden Boy. Ha!" He tipped back in his chair and placed his hands behind his head, revealing large damp spots under both arms.

I didn't know how to respond so I continued to look at him steadily without saying anything.

Flustered, he sat forward again and leaned his elbows on the edge of his desk. Then he opened his drawer slightly, pulled out a pair of nail clippers and began to clip as he spoke.

"Evan thought he was real hot stuff, you know? He got by on personality, and pretty soon everyone thought he was a real up-and-comer. He just drew everybody in with his act, including the head honchos around here, but the truth is he wasn't all that smart or that good. Some of the rest of us were working our butts off over in the corner, but nobody noticed us. Oh, no. They were too busy being dazzled by lover boy."

Wes finally looked at me, and I was shaken by the raw anger and loathing in his eyes. I hadn't the slightest suspicion of the abhorrence he felt toward Evan. But then it was true that when Evan was around, someone like Wes faded into the woodwork. He'd been so overshadowed by the force of Evan's personality that he must have felt like a cipher.

"So you're saying there was a lot of resentment?" I said, the understatement of the year to hear Wes tell it. I was learning how difficult it would be to question people about Evan when I had cared so much about him. How could I be objective about what they told me? How could I conceal my disgust of Wes? I willed myself not to let any emotion show.

He laid down the clippers, leaned back and crossed his arms on top of his belly. He looked as though he was about to give a final argument to a jury, all puffed up and full of self-importance. "Exactly right. And I'll tell you something else about Evan. I thought he was on the take."

I momentarily lost my cool in spite of my determination not to. "You can't be serious. Whatever would give you such an idea?" It took a lot of self-discipline not to say "*extremely ridiculous* idea." I could feel a muscle pulsating in my right eyebrow. It had a way of going into spasms when I was really tense, and right now I was so uptight it was a wonder my whole body wasn't jerking visibly.

"The guy lived way beyond his means. Some of our senior partners earn enough to live like that, but Evan was only with the firm for five years, and Chris doesn't work. Now you tell me how he could afford a place at the country club. It's all I can do to afford a halfway decent apartment. Not only that, they traveled a lot, and they weren't visiting Disneyland, either. They were going to Monaco and Hawaii and Switzerland. Would you believe he got himself a Rolex a couple of months ago? Come on."

I knew for a fact it was a fake Rolex. Evan had told me about it the night of the Girl Scout dinner, saying he'd gotten it to shake up the guys at the firm. Apparently he did just that. I wasn't about to spoil the joke now.

"Maybe he or Chris inherited money," I suggested.

"No way. His mother is still alive and his father was a schoolteacher. I don't think his wife's family had money, either."

Chris had told me once that most of what they had was owned by the bank. Apparently Wes never thought of that. But I wasn't going to betray any confidences, so I didn't bother to point out that possibility to him. He was going to see conspiracy where Evan was concerned no matter what I said.

"Do you have anything else to add?" I asked as benignly as I could manage.

Wes seemed disappointed that he hadn't gotten more of a rise out of me. "Just that I can understand why Bernard decided to blow him away. Not that I would have gone that far myself. I do respect the law. But I always fantasized about how I could bring him down legally. Now I don't have to."

I stood up, forcing myself to maintain a calm

appearance. "I guess that about covers it. Thank you for your help, Wes."

He rose halfway from his chair as I left, plopping down in it before I got out of the room.

When I finally got into my car and shut the door, I said aloud, "Yes, thanks, Wes, you schmuck, you."

TWELVE

AS I DROVE AWAY from the law offices, I was angry and not sure where that anger was directed. Was it at Annalee and Wes, or was it toward myself? I knew Evan wasn't perfect; he was human wasn't he? But was I so gullible that I had failed to see that he was a womanizer and/or unethical lawyer? I thought I could size people up with a high degree of accuracy. And he had always seemed so straight arrow to me. Had I been completely taken in? Damn it all, why was I thinking like this? These people were jealous of his success, or in Annalee's case, his lack of attention. If they couldn't hurt him when he was alive, they'd stoop to smearing him in death. Wouldn't they? I was really concerned now. How could I ever arrive at a totally objective viewpoint where Evan was concerned?

I called the Scout office on my cell phone and

asked to speak to Latoya. “It’s Tommi. Got plans for lunch?” I asked when she answered.

“I’ve got a wonderful peanut butter sandwich I brought from home. Care to share it?”

“Think you could pass it up for a salad at the Moose Café over at Farmer’s Market? I’m buying.”

“My goodness. To what do I owe this special treat?” Latoya asked.

“Just need to bounce some things off you. Is twelve-thirty okay?”

“Sounds pretty mysterious. You know I can’t resist an invitation like that. See you then.”

Latoya was already seated at a table when I arrived. We both ordered chicken caesar salads and made small talk until they arrived. I focused on Latoya’s earrings while composing my thoughts. They were made from tiny, various-colored Indian beads and hung in three tiers almost touching her shoulders.

“Okay,” said Latoya, “You’ve stalled long enough. Let’s hear it. It’s about Bernard, isn’t it? I almost called you when I saw it in the paper this morning, but I overslept and was late to work. How do you feel about it?”

“I’m positive he didn’t do it.”

Latoya smiled a slight smile and drummed her

fingers on the table for a minute before she spoke. "I sort of expected you to say 'serves the so-and-so right.'"

I shook my head. "I've gotta admit when Evan said he was suing him for malpractice, I thought he was getting his just deserts. I loved the idea of him getting his comeuppance. But not this, Latoya. I lived with him for many years, and I know he's not a murderer. A jerk sometimes, yes, but not a killer."

"So where do I come in?"

"You're not going to believe this, but Pamela has asked me to help them."

Latoya looked even more surprised than I had anticipated. "You're putting me on," she said.

"No, 'fraid not."

"Why you of all people?"

"Pamela's desperate. I think she's deluding herself if she thinks I can do anything, but she really got to me. And I want to find out who really killed Evan. It doesn't look like the cops are going to look any further."

"You never cease to amaze me."

"Well, I'll tell you the truth, Latoya, it's more exciting than answering phones and filing. It could get addictive."

"I can see it now, a little cubbyhole with a sign on the door, 'Tommi Poag, Private Investigator.'"

I laughed. "Not hardly, no. I'd never do it for a living. But I can still ask questions, and I suppose I'm a natural snoop. When I was in school, I always had the reputation of knowing everything about everybody. People just seem to open up to me. I think it's because they know I'll keep their secret. Or maybe it's just this sweet li'l face of mine invites confession," I said, fluttering my eyelashes and clasping my hands under my chin in an angelic pose.

"Sweet? Ha!"

"That's our little secret, Latoya. Besides, how would you know from sweet?"

"No comment."

"Anyway, the whole point of this lunch is to ask you if you thought Evan could have been having an affair with one of the Girl Scout staff."

Latoya chewed thoughtfully on a piece of chicken. "I know lots of people who thought Evan was pretty cool, but as far as I'm concerned all the flirting was strictly in fun. I never heard a whisper that he had anything going with any of them. So either there's been a conspiracy of silence at the office—and I very much doubt that since it would be a first—or no one has heard anything."

I shrugged in frustration. "I've been told things about Evan that are hard to believe. I don't know what to think anymore."

"Like what? And how reliable is the source?"

"It was his secretary who told me she thought he was having an affair. And another lawyer in Evan's firm tried to tell me Evan was probably involved in something illegal."

"No way. He wasn't the type."

"That's what I think. But am I kidding myself? I've got to know for sure. Maybe he got killed because he was mixed up in something shady."

"Shady, shmady. You can't tell me Evan McCandless was crooked. Don't sweat it, Tommi." Latoya was studying the menu again as if the subject were closed. "Have you ever tried their pecan pie?"

"Please don't tempt me." I spent most of my life in the battle of the bulge.

Latoya flagged down the waitress and ordered the pie. "Don't let Pamela drag you into this," she said after the waitress left. "Bernard is innocent. They won't be able to hang it on him. Forget about it, and just remember the good times you had with

Evan and ignore all this other stuff they're saying which is nothing but evil gossip."

I felt better after talking with Latoya. But I couldn't agree with her about Bernard's fate. Innocent people were sometimes wrongfully jailed or even executed.

When I left the restaurant, I drove to Battleground Park close to my condo. It's the site of a decisive battle during the Revolutionary War where General Greene, although he lost to the British forces, decimated their ranks which led to their ultimate defeat. It's a lovely park that, although surrounded by housing developments, gives the illusion of being away from it all. I walked to a bench where Bernard and I used to sit during the Sunday evening concerts every summer. Near the west entrance of the park azaleas still bloomed in the heavy shade though most others in town had already faded. It was quiet now. Only the hum of insects was superimposed over the chatter of birds.

It was such a perfect day, and I felt so unutterably sad. Was it really true that the good die young?

All I wanted to do was sit there for the rest of the afternoon and watch the robins make a nest in the sweet gum tree nearby. I wanted to think about new beginnings, not endings. But my mind wouldn't cooperate. It kept wanting to go its own way, and its way was to go back to the puzzle of Evan's death.

THIRTEEN

I'D BEEN VERY CONCERNED about Melanie the day that Evan was killed, but there'd been no opportunity yet to check on her. Melanie was one of those supersensitive souls who had a harder time than most dealing with life's vicissitudes. I wasn't that far from her neighborhood, so I decided to drop by and see her.

As I expected, Melanie was home when I called her.

She had two preschoolers as well as a second-grader. Even though she admitted it was not easy to live on Ty's salary alone, Melanie had no intention of going to work until her youngest was in school. She and I had discussed working mothers on various occasions, and she was quite inflexible in her views about leaving toddlers in day care.

When I parked in front of the Tyler's modest ranch in Garden Homes, I could see Melanie standing inside the front door watching for me, cradling eight-month-old Brian on her hip while three-year-old Annie clung to her legs.

The small living room was to the left of the tiny foyer, and when I entered it I saw Ty sitting in a recliner reading a spy novel. He got up and extended his hand to me. "Good to see you, Tommi."

"I'm sorry, I didn't realize it was your day off, Ty. I'd have come another time."

"No problem. Besides I wanted to tell you how sorry I was about Evan. He was a stand-up guy, and I know you two had become close. And then Bernard's arrest had to come as a shock to you. Melanie tells me his wife has asked you to help him out. That's generous of you, considering."

I almost regretted having told Melanie about Pamela's request when I called her. Why did everyone seem to have a problem with that? I was tired of having to defend my decision. And I wasn't anxious for anyone in the police department to know what I was doing, even though the investigation was being conducted by the sheriff since the killing happened outside the city limits. They would no doubt think I was way out of line. If not downright crazy. I should have thought of that before sharing information with Melanie.

"Well, let her sit down before we talk," interrupted Melanie steering me toward the couch. I had to pick my way through a jumble of toys.

"How about some Coke?" Melanie asked as she sat Brian on the rug.

"Fine," I said. I had just come from lunch, but I didn't want to deny Melanie a chance to play hostess. She didn't get to do that very often.

"You even get a choice of Girl Scout cookies."

"Great. Do you know I haven't had one since I gave up my troop? There aren't any young people around me. I've really missed those chocolate mints." I'd resisted the pie at the Moose Cafe, hadn't I?

When Melanie left the room, Annie sidled up to me, stood in front of me with a finger in her mouth and looking down at the floor said, "Hi," shyly twisting her shoulders first one way then the other.

"Hi, yourself. And how old are you?"

Still gazing at the floor, Annie held up three chubby fingers. I was hooked.

Melanie returned with Coke, cookies and a bottle, which Brian sucked on with noisy satisfaction. Annie chewed on a peanut butter cookie as she sat on the floor putting together a jigsaw puzzle made of simple animal shapes. She would glance surreptitiously at me from time to time to make sure she had an audience.

"I just wondered how you were doing, Melanie," I said. "I was concerned about you last Saturday."

Melanie frowned. "That has to be one of the worst days of my life. It haunts me to think I was the last one to talk to him."

"You didn't catch a glimpse of Bernard out there, did you?"

"No, all I saw were the people who had volunteered for the exercise and the girls."

"It doesn't make sense to me," I said almost to myself. "If Bernard had decided to kill Evan, which is ridiculous in itself, why would he go out to camp to do it?"

"I haven't heard much about the investigation yet because we're not handling it," Ty said, "but the theory is that he knew Evan was in the exercise and decided that it was his best chance to get away with killing him and making it look accidental. So he must have gone out there and hung around hoping to see him."

"But how would he know Evan was going to be

there?" I asked. "It wasn't like they were pals and Evan was going to call him up and tell him about it."

"Was there some kind of notice in the paper?" Ty reached over and took three cookies from the plate.

"Now that you mention it, there was. That Celeste person who does the social column wrote about the upcoming exercise and named some of the people who were going to be in it, at least those who are routinely in the society news." I didn't mention that Latoya told me they'd hoped for serious coverage of the disaster exercise to highlight the good work the girls were doing, but not a reporter showed up until Evan was killed.

Annie finished her puzzle and came over to me and bashfully pointed to her accomplishment.

"Very good, Annie. Such a smart girl." I patted her cheek.

"Why don't you do another one?" her mother said, and Annie hurried off to her toys.

"How's Chris doing?" Melanie asked.

"About as you would imagine. Pretty broken up. The worst thing is that the insurance investigator insinuated she might be involved somehow. As if losing Evan wasn't enough."

"You mean the guy who was robbed and killed?"

"Yes, wasn't that unreal? A little hard to swallow that it was simply a robbery." I was still having trouble believing that.

"They haven't found any evidence to suggest it was anything else," Ty said.

"Well, why on earth would he have been suspicious of Chris?" Melanie asked.

"When an insurance company stands to lose a million and a half bucks, the beneficiary always looks suspicious to them." Ty must have known that from experience.

Melanie's mouth dropped open. "Wow. That is a lot of money. Maybe Chris isn't as bereaved as she leads everyone to believe."

"Melanie!" I couldn't believe she'd said that.

"Just kidding." Melanie said it lightly, but the look on her face told me she was still considering it. Melanie did not know Chris well. She wouldn't know how much in love they were, and how devastated Chris was by his death.

I stood up. "Well, I need to be going."

"Come back any time, Tommi," Ty said, arising from his chair. "Let us know if there is anything we can do to help."

"Thanks," I said. I waved to the children as I left. "Bye, kids."

Annie smiled and waved back, but Brian was too busy with a terry cloth ball to notice. I felt a wince of longing as I walked to my car. I had gone through a phase when I was first married when I cried every time I had a period and realized I wasn't pregnant. That ache lasted for years before it finally diminished, though it never went away entirely. Now I was at the age when my friends all had grandchildren, which brought the pain and disappointment to the fore all over again.

FOURTEEN

MELANIE'S COMMENT MADE ME realize I had to talk to Chris, much as I hated to cause her any more pain. When I called her at home, she seemed eager to see me. I figured she must now be at the point in her grief where she no longer wanted to be alone but needed to be with friends. She greeted me at the door wearing designer jeans and an oversize T-shirt with the logo of her alma mater, Peace College. After hugging me, she stepped back and took hold of my hand. "I know it's awkward for you, Tommi. When I heard about Bernard, I couldn't believe my ears."

"That's only half of it, Chris."

"What do you mean?"

"Pamela has asked me to help him."

"Help him? How?"

"You may not know this, but I solved a murder Bernard was working on about a year ago. She hopes I can do that again."

"Ooh." Chris's seemed unsure of what to say. "You're convinced he didn't do it, then."

"Absolutely. I'll tell you the truth, I feel damned uncomfortable when I have to ask my friends sticky questions. I'm not sure why I agreed to this, but I guess Pamela pushed all the right buttons. And I believe he's innocent."

Chris was silent for a moment as she stood thoughtfully looking off into space. "I don't know him at all. But I certainly accept your judgment on that, Tommi. Still, it doesn't look too good for him right now, does it?"

"Well, the sheriff is convinced he's guilty. And I haven't as yet found out anything that would change his mind. But I've only started."

Chris took my hand and squeezed it. "Good luck, then." She waved toward the living room. "Have a seat if you can find one. The living room's a mess right now because I'm in the midst of spring cleaning."

The normally picture-perfect living room was in a state of great disarray. The drapes were gone, all the knickknacks were missing from the tables, the chair cushions had been pulled out and were stacked in the corner, and there was a cluster of bottles on the mantle containing cleaners and waxes along with brushes, rags and sponges. A shop vacuum cleaner sat beside a chair, the crevice tool still inserted into the space between the seat and the arm. I tried to imagine what I might find in the crevices of my own furniture and shuddered at the thought.

"Good lord," I said, "your house looked perfect to me. Why are you knocking yourself out like this?"

Chris smiled, the first time I'd seen her do so since Evan's death. "Don't you know this is therapy for me? When I'm down, I'd rather scrub a floor than do anything else."

"When you run out of floors here, I've got some sinfully dirty ones for you."

"Thanks, anyway. I get those kind of offers frequently, but I manage to resist."

"Darn."

"Something to drink?"

I was going to float away soon but accepted, anyway. I'd learned that women relaxed a little, lowered their guard if they were put in the role of hostess. Then questioning took on a guise of natural chitchat.

While Chris was in the kitchen, I looked around

the room. She was evidently the type who dismantled everything when she cleaned. I hit only the most visible places and don't worry too much about the parts that don't show. But then Chris and Evan had filled their home with costly furnishings. It was no wonder she took such good care of them. Was it true what she had said about the bank owning much of it? I wondered if the insurance policy was crucial to her being able to remain here. Were there other assets? It wasn't the kind of question you could normally ask a friend, but I needed to know.

Chris returned carrying two iced teas. "Hope you don't mind instant. It's all I have."

"That's fine." I hate instant.

"So, have you found out anything?"

"I need to tell you exactly what I'm doing, Chris. I don't want you to think I'm overstepping my bounds."

"I don't understand what you mean." Chris stirred her tea and carefully laid her spoon on a piece of newspaper to protect the top of the coffee table. She had provided a coaster for each of our glasses, and when moisture rolled off the side of her glass and ran over the edge of the coaster, she quickly grabbed a rag and wiped it up before it could harm the finish. I was so afraid of damaging the table that I continued to hold my glass, unwilling to set it down.

"I've been talking to people about Evan and his relationships to others." I took a quick sip of tea, waiting to see how Chris would react.

Chris ran her finger up and down the side of her glass, tracing lines through the moisture. She did not look at me. Finally, she said in a low voice, "And what did they say?"

"For one thing there are rumors of another woman." Damn, I hated doing this. But Bernard's life was more important than Evan's reputation.

Chris's hand gripping the glass started to shake, and she looked as if she was going to cry. Her tea was sloshing onto the pale gray carpeting, but she was unaware of it.

Feeling like a jerk I added, "I emphasize the word rumors."

Chris finally looked at me. Though the pain was evident in her eyes, she forced a half smile and tried for a tone of flippancy as she said, "And just who is the lucky lady supposed to be?"

"That's just it. I haven't got a name. It's probably a figment of someone's imagination."

Chris finally set down her glass directly on the highly-polished cherry table. I picked it up and put it on her coaster and wiped up the droplets it left. Chris didn't seem to notice.

"That makes it even worse," Chris said. "I'd at least like to have someone in particular to hate."

"Do you think there's something to those rumors?" I wondered if I would be able to sense whether Chris was being truthful. A vehement denial might mean she really suspected something.

Chris shrugged her shoulders with resignation. "What can I say? The wife is always the last to find out." She blushed suddenly and patted my hand. "Oh, sorry, I forgot. That was just a general statement."

"Don't apologize. I know only too well."

"I've got to admit that I'd worried a lot since he hired Annalee. She's sharp and good-looking, and they were together so much of the day. There was probably nothing to it, but he did work awfully long hours sometimes."

"Just like every other lawyer in the universe. What about somebody else? Do you think he was interested in anyone connected with the Girl Scouts?"

"The Girl Scouts!" Chris looked incredulous. "That idea never crossed my mind." She stared out the window. "The Girl Scouts," she muttered to herself several times. "You know," she finally continued. "Now that you mention it, he was always awfully eager to go to Girl Scout functions, like the Disaster Day thing. He talked about it a lot."

"Maybe he just thought it would be a fun thing to do. It wasn't the sort of event that lent itself to hanky panky. Everyone was too busy being involved with the exercise."

Chris buried her face in her hands briefly. When she looked up at me again, her look was serious and determined. "Why am I even considering infidelity? Why has his death cast so much doubt on everything? I say I worried about Annalee, but truly, Tommi, he was always so loving and attentive it's shameful to have any doubts. I'm sure he was faithful. I can't believe anything else."

I wished I could end the conversation at that point, but I couldn't.

"Chris," I said, "I don't want to belabor all of these rumors, but I do need to ask. Someone suggested he might have been involved in something illegal at work that was bringing in big bucks."

"What!" Chris jumped to her feet in anger. "It's one thing to say he was having an affair, but quite another to say he was crooked. Who told you this?"

"I can't tell you that. I'm sorry."

Chris was pounding her fist on the mantel now. "I bet I know. It was that wimpy tub of lard Wesley, wasn't it? He's always been jealous of Evan. To think he'd smear his name after he's dead. I can't believe it." She broke down crying again.

I got up to comfort her. "Sorry I had to ask that."

Chris soon regained her composure. "I want to show you something, Tommi. Wait here a minute." She ran out of the room and up the stairs. In a few minutes she was back down again, carrying a well-worn accordion pleated file folder. She sat down beside me on the sofa.

"Look," she said, untying the string that held the file closed at the top and spilling the contents onto the damask cushions of the sofa. She sorted through the papers until she found a small booklet. "Here's the mortgage payment record." She opened it to where the last entry had been made. It showed a payment of $3495 for the month of May with a balance of $439,737.23 on the mortgage.

"And here," she said, picking up a bank statement. She opened it and handed it to me. It showed a balance of $1482.78 in a savings account.

"If Evan was on the take, don't you think he would have paid off the mortgage! That thirty-five hundred a month is a killer to pay. Wouldn't we have more than a paltry fifteen hundred dollars in the savings account? I told you we lived up to and over the hilt." She waved her hand around indicating the room. "The fact is, even with the insurance money, I'll probably have to sell it. I just can't continue to live the way we did. I'm going to have to invest the money for income because I could never find a decent job. Frankly, I haven't any damn skills. I'd be doing well to make minimum wage. Can't you just see me at McDonald's flipping hamburgers?" She began to laugh hysterically.

I sat quietly till she calmed down. "You didn't need to do that," I said.

"Yes, I did," Chris retorted. "So you can go tell Wesley he's a lying son of a bitch, and you can tell him how you know."

"I will if you want me to, but why not ignore him?"

"How can you ignore a poisonous snake? He'll have a good laugh over the fact that Evan was head over heels in debt, but that's a damn sight better than having him spread vicious lies about him."

FIFTEEN

THE LAST THING I wanted to do was to face Wesley again; I found him utterly repugnant. But after Chris's emotional outpouring, I felt I had to do what I could to stop his ugly rumors about Evan. He was probably blabbing his allegations to anyone who would listen.

I didn't bother to call ahead but drove straight to the law office hoping to find Wesley there. He was.

He rose halfheartedly from his chair when the secretary showed me in, then slumped back into his seat.

"Did you come to ask more about Evan?" he asked with an air of deliberately transparent naïveté.

I pulled my chair up close to his desk so I could lean upon it and stare at him at close range. I could play the intimidation game myself. He pulled himself back in his big leather chair, flustered for the moment.

"No," I said. "I've come to tell you you're full of beans to put it politely. I've just come from Chris's, and she showed me her mortgage payment book and savings passbook. They've been living right up to the hilt and then some. If he's on the take as you claim, they'd have paid everything off a long time ago. I think it's time you retracted your stories about him. I have a feeling you've been telling them to anyone who'd listen."

Wesley didn't deny it. He pulled himself up to his desk and lowered his head to stare back at me, not the least bit penitent. "That's no damn proof. He could have been socking it away in the islands or Switzerland or something, just waiting till he had a really good stash so he could disappear and leave his debts behind. He didn't want to arouse suspicion by paying everything off."

"If he didn't want to raise suspicions, then he wouldn't have bought a house in Irving Park," I countered.

Wesley broke into a slow smile as if he'd been awaiting that particular statement. He almost glowed with smugness. "Oh, I think he'd already done that. I think he first got himself in over his head and then got involved in whatever, because he couldn't extricate himself otherwise."

I was amazed at his self-righteousness. He clung to the idea of Evan's guilt as though making him look bad would somehow elevate his own position. What a sorry human being he was.

"You haven't offered one shred of evidence," I said, "and you are destroying people's lives with your flights of fancy. Don't you have any compassion for Chris?"

"They never gave a damn about me. Why should I care about her? I'm just telling it like it is." He sat back looking pleased with himself.

"You're only telling it like you wish it were. I guess I'm wasting my time." I rose to leave. "Do me a favor, though. Give it a rest for now. If there's any truth in what you're saying, the authorities will find out about it."

He lumbered to his feet to escort me from the office. "Oh, they will, they will."

I couldn't get out of there fast enough. I knew I had wasted my time trying to reason with him. I felt drained and depressed, and since it was now after four, I could accomplish little more today. I drove back to my condo, stopping at the supermarket on the way, and changed into my most comfortable jeans and my Camp Galimore sweatshirt. Poor Camp Galimore. Would it ever be the same?

I lay on the sofa after consuming most of a frozen pizza reading a trashy gossip magazine I'd picked up on impulse at the checkout counter. Although I often was curious about what lay behind the outrageous headlines that always caught my eye as I stood in line, I was too embarrassed to buy one. This time I didn't give a damn what anybody thought. Just as junk food always helped when I felt low, I thought a little junk reading might be a distraction. But even the stories about aliens from space and ten-year-old newlyweds couldn't keep my mind from straying. Annalee's allegations kept nipping at the heels of my attention like yapping little mutts. Who on earth at the Girl Scouts could have been involved with Evan. If there was any truth to it. And then I thought of Mary Ellen Jones. A young black woman, she was confined to a wheelchair because of a back injury she suffered as an infant. She had been the receptionist at the Girl Scout office for the past six years and knew more about everyone in the council than anyone else. She could draw information out of people with the slickness a magician employed to pull rabbits out of a hat. And she did it before you were aware of it. Mary Ellen knew things about you that you wouldn't want to divulge to your best friend. And if she could do that with volunteers, God knew what she'd learned about the staff who were around all of the time. Yet she never talked about these private matters; she kept it all very much to herself. Which is why, I supposed, no one minded telling her things. She served as the informal in-house shrink and people often used her as a sounding board.

I called Mary Ellen at her apartment which was part of a HUD-sponsored complex built especially for the disabled and elderly, and where all her neighbors were retirees. She refused to let them "sit on their asses for the rest of their lives," and had organized a choir and kitchen band and generally kept the place humming. I knew she stayed busy in the evenings and weekends and was pleasantly surprised when Mary Ellen answered the phone.

"Hi, it's Tommi Poag." Since I'd seen Mary Ellen on Monday when I visited the Girl Scout office, I didn't have to remind her who I was. Not that she was likely to forget.

"Hey, what's happening?"

"Well, this has to do with Evan's death and my ex-husband, Bernard. I guess you heard they arrested him."

"Yeah, that kinda surprised me. I don't know

him, but if you used to be married to him, he must be okay."

Bless Mary Ellen. "I'm trying to help him out if I can. So I'm going to ask you some questions you might not want to answer. But it's important. Do you know if Evan called anyone on the staff an unusual number of times?"

Mary Ellen said nothing for a minute. "I don't really like to talk about private stuff."

"I wouldn't ordinarily ask you about something like this—" I was thinking that the council was fortunate to have someone so discreet in that position "—but maybe the information could help Bernard. I want to follow up on some rumors I've been hearing. It might not amount to anything important, but I have to check out every little thing. You understand that, don't you?"

"Well, okay, as long as you keep it to yourself."

"Of course, if it hasn't anything to do with the case. But if it should prove to be evidence, then I'd have to share it with the sheriff. But you want to help Bernard, don't you?"

"Sure, Tommi. It's just that I keep what I see and hear to myself to hang on to my job. I know they'd can me quick if they thought I ran my mouth about things at the office that are no one else's business."

"Don't worry about that. I won't let you get into any trouble."

"Well, okay, if you say so." She sounded not quite convinced and paused for a minute before continuing. "He called Barb Kellerman a lot."

I was speechless. The Camp Director? The one I'd talked to in Latoya's office last Monday morning? Her shock and surprise over Evan's killing seemed in line with every one else's—the sort of response one would have at the death of an acquaintance. She certainly hadn't reacted as though he'd been her lover. In fact, she seemed mostly concerned about the camping program.

"Are you there?" Mary Ellen asked.

"I'm here. Anyone else?" I hoped I sounded composed.

"Oh, he talked to all the Field Directors now and then. I suppose it was about the cookie sale."

"But he called Barb the most."

"Yep."

"Well, thanks a lot, Mary Ellen. I appreciate your help."

"Glad to. Come see us when you can."

When I hung up I tried to imagine Barbara and Evan together. It wasn't a far-fetched notion. Barb had patrician looks—a Roman nose and high cheekbones—which she matched with enormous style. Her husband was a popular dentist so she could afford to dress well, and her clothes were understated and elegant. I always had supposed that camp directors were tomboy types who wore only shorts or blue jeans, but Barb dressed in tailored designer clothes when in the office. And she had an efficient no-nonsense management style that had improved the camp facilities and program enormously since she'd taken the job. That was why it was particularly tragic when it appeared that the summer program might have to be cancelled.

It was hard to accept the notion that Evan might have been seeing Barb. If it turned out that he was but it had no bearing on his death, should I tell Chris? I didn't think so. What purpose would it serve but to hurt her? With these question on my mind, I called Barb and arranged to have lunch with her the next day.

SIXTEEN

I HAD ANOTHER restless night. In desperation I even ejected Tee from my bed although he had barely stirred. It was a waste of energy, though, because he stood outside my bedroom door meowing pitifully until I let him in again. I tossed and turned several more hours before finally falling into a deep sleep around five o'clock. At ten o'clock I woke with a start feeling hungover. I couldn't go back to sleep but didn't want to sit home marking time for the next hour and a half. So I donned my running suit (which I consider a major misnomer because I never, ever run) and went out for a brisk walk. My condo is in an area of many condominium and apartment complexes and affords sidewalks which is more than you can say for most of the neighborhoods in town newer than forty years old. Walking is the extent of my keeping in shape except for my yoga classes that are more for my psyche than my body.

I walked around heavily wooded areas lining Cottage Place and listened to the mockingbirds as they trilled their entire repertoire over and over as if practicing for a songbird competition. It was a day that belied all the sorrow and tragedy of the world.

When I got home, I dressed carefully in a two-piece dress of pastel colors that resembled an abstract watercolor. I wanted to make sure I looked at least as good as Barb. I couldn't explain it, but it had something to do with feeling in control of the situation. Although clothes meant far less to me now than they used to, I knew that if I felt tacky next to someone who was impeccably dressed, it affected my self-confidence.

Barb wasn't there when I got to the Moose Cafe so I let the hostess seat me near the front window and ordered coffee. Maybe the caffeine would give me a much needed lift. It was ten minutes later when Barb arrived, and it seemed to me that she, too, had put extra effort into her appearance. She was wearing a beautiful silk noil shirtwaist dress in powder blue.

"Sorry," she said as she breezed into the other

chair. "The phone never stops ringing. I can't get any work done."

"What's the verdict? Are you going to be able to hold camp?"

Barb ran her index fingers wearily up and down her temples. She looked tireder than I had ever seen her. "I don't know yet. Things are starting to turn around some. This sounds terrible, Tommi, but since they arrested Bernard, some parents are changing their minds. I guess they feel that if he's in jail, there's no danger anymore."

"There's a problem with that since I'm sure he didn't do it," I said.

"Well, I can understand how you feel. But don't you think you might be a bit prejudiced?"

"No, Barb, I don't." I thought her tone was just a bit deprecating.

The waitress came then, and we studied our menus intently. I ordered spinach quiche and Barb asked for seafood salad.

"Now," Barb said when he left, "what's on your mind?"

I struggled to get the right tone in my voice. I didn't want to be abrasive and turn Barb off, but I wanted the question to sound authoritative enough to elicit an answer. It was tough when you had no prerogative to make someone respond. Well, come to think of it, even the police couldn't make someone talk. But their questioning would certainly be more compelling.

"Is it true that Evan called you often?"

Barb maintained the same expression, but her eyes grew wary. "And just where did you hear that?" Her voice had an edge to it she couldn't disguise.

"Around."

Barb stared at me. "I want to know."

"I'm sorry, but I can't say."

Her face suddenly softened. "Oh, well," she shrugged, "I guess there's no reason I can't tell you."

Thank God for that.

"Evan did call me quite a bit. Actually, we knew each other long before he got involved with the Girl Scouts. We both grew up in Franklin, in the mountains, you know—" I didn't know "—and we were in the same class in high school. We weren't close then, we ran with different crowds, but I guess he needed a confidante lately, and since he'd known me earlier, he'd call me up and pour out his soul. He was the kind of guy who was really more comfortable with women than with men. He could talk to us more easily. And he found out I would listen and sympathize."

"What was bothering him?"

Barb looked at me thoughtfully, and finally spoke. "I don't know if I should say this or not, considering you are good friends with Chris."

"I'll keep it in strictest confidence. You know that."

"Well, Chris was making him miserable. She was spending his money like crazy, and he was up to his eyeballs in debt. And she was sure he was being unfaithful and hounding him about it. So he'd call me up and cry on my shoulder."

I found this hard to swallow. Someone for sure wasn't telling the truth. Was it Chris or Barb?

The waitress appeared with our plates, and we said nothing as she fussed over us.

"Are you saying Chris was the spendthrift?" I asked when she finally left. "I had the impression it was the other way around." It was a struggle to maintain a facade of indifference.

"That's what he told me. He was really worried about their financial situation."

"So there was nothing between you two."

"Not hardly." Barb laughed. "I was just upset that anyone was taking notes on who I talked to and how often."

"Well, I did hear rumors that he was having an affair. If he talked to you a lot, I was hoping he might have mentioned who it was."

Barb said nothing but gave a smug smile as if to say, *Oh sure, Tommi, I really believe that you meant he was seeing someone other than me.*

After Barb returned to the office, I remained at the table going over the conversation in my mind. I'd always considered Barb to be honest, but then I'd always thought that about Chris, as well. One of them was not telling the truth. Was Barb making this all up to cover up the fact she'd been having an affair with Evan? Perhaps she'd suspected what I wanted to talk to her about and had rehearsed her story so that she could tell it so convincingly.

On the other hand, what if Barb was telling the truth? Could Chris be the way Barb had pictured her: jealous and possessive and demanding more and more things that they couldn't afford? If it were true, it could have been a motive to kill Evan. Surely Carter Raines couldn't have been right about her. But then why would Chris say she'd have to sell the house? Why show me the bills? If she were overspending, why kill her meal ticket? Unless she needed the insurance money.

SEVENTEEN

After Barb's revelation, I wondered if I really knew Chris after all. Upon analysis, I realized it was only Evan that I had known well. We had seen each other often during the divorce proceedings and had lunch occasionally since. I saw Chris only sporadically at social functions when there were many other people around, and it was impossible to get to know each other intimately.

I'd even begun to question my image of Evan after all I'd heard these past couple of days. It was becoming apparent that individuals are not made up of a given set of personality traits. Instead, it is how you are perceived by others that matters. And those perceptions can be different for everyone who knows you. It's like looking in a fun house mirror. The size and shape of the image depends on where the viewer is standing. And everyone is looking at the image in the mirror from a different perspective.

Speaking of perspective, what about my view of Bernard? It could hardly be unbiased. If only I could erase all my feelings toward him and approach this puzzle with a clean slate of emotions: no hurt, no anger, not even any twinges of long-lost desire. Simply react as if I had never known him, as though he had just come into my life and I knew nothing about him.

Impossible.

I DROVE TO THE Sheriff's Department on Washington Street. Perhaps I could learn what Deputy Kronenberger knew about the case if he was willing to share it with me. He was the one I'd gone to at camp when I found Evan's body. Maybe that would give me an "in."

I had to wait for ten minutes on a miserably uncomfortable bench in the hallway watching people drift in and out. Finally, Kronenberger appeared behind the reception counter and gave me a wave. "Mrs. Poag, good to see you. Come on back to my office."

He lifted a section of the countertop to let me through and led the way down several corridors to a cluttered room that held three desks, a row of file cabinets, and had the look of sorely overtaxed space that could barely contain the amount of work taking place there.

There certainly wasn't an iota of grace or cordiality to these rooms, but it wasn't the kind of place that was meant to give comfort. Intimidation would normally be the name of the game here. I thought it was as depressing as a place should be that deals mainly with the darker side of humanity.

"Have a seat." The deputy directed me to the chair beside a desk. What would it be like to be sitting there under different circumstances? Were only victims questioned here? Was there an even more unpleasant room than this, where the suspects were interrogated? I wondered if it was anything like the way it happened in the movies, harsh lights shining directly in the eyes, tough-looking officers chewing on cigars and barking questions at the suspect. Of course, I was thinking of the movies Bernard liked to rent starring James Cagney and Humphrey Bogart. Maybe they tried to sweet-talk them into confessing now. But I doubted it.

"What can I do for you?" Kronenberger asked.

"Pamela Poag, Bernard's wife, has asked me to help them out. I don't have any official status. I'm not working for his lawyer, but I hoped maybe you could fill me in on the charges." I didn't see any reason to tell him that I'd once been married to Bernard myself. Though he probably already knew that.

Kronenberger chewed on his lip thoughtfully. "Can't really tell you much except what's been given to the media. His lawyer, of course, is entitled to all we've got, but since you're not on his staff.... This is kind of an unusual situation you know."

I started to rise. "In that case..."

"Since it'll be on TV tonight I guess I can tell you he's been charged in Raines's death, too."

"Oh, my God!" I sank back into the chair. "I can't believe this."

"They found Mr. Poag's gun in a trash bin downtown. It had been used to kill Carter Raines, and it had his fingerprints on it."

"Well, of course it would have his prints if it belonged to him. Weren't there any others?"

"The man who found it is all."

I closed my eyes trying to recall what the article in the paper had said when Bernard was arrested. "Didn't I read that the rifle used to shoot Evan had all the fingerprints wiped off?"

"That's right. It was clean."

"Then why wouldn't he have wiped them off the pistol, too? It doesn't make sense."

"We think he panicked when he heard someone coming right after he shot Raines, so he tossed it into the trash bin and ran, thinking that the trash would get picked up and no one would ever find it. Unfortunately for him, a homeless man was digging through it looking for food. When he came across it, he had the good sense to turn it in. Maybe he thought he'd get a reward."

"And how do you know he wasn't the one who killed Raines?"

"Because he was sleeping at the Salvation Army building at that time. Several people vouched for him."

"What about Bernard? Doesn't he have an alibi? I understand it was pretty early in the morning." I knew I was pushing the boundaries on my questions, but as long as he kept answering, I was going to keep asking. It probably would all be in the paper, anyway.

"He tried a real doozy of an alibi. Claims the night before Raines's death someone called who said he'd just split from his wife and had to fly across country early the next morning for an interview in California. This guy wanted to make sure his will was changed before he left because he was so scared of flying. He begged Poag to meet him at the law office very early in the a.m. And Poag swears he sat in his car for an hour in front of the building, but the guy never showed up. No one can verify he was there. Pretty imaginative, don't you think?"

"I don't think Bernard has that much imagination. Couldn't it have been a setup?"

"We've got to go with the evidence. And at this time, it all points toward him. I'm sorry for you, and I'm sorry for his wife. But we have to call it the way we see it."

"I understand. Anything else you can tell me?"

"That's all we can make public."

"Okay. Well, thanks for sharing that much with me."

Deputy Kronenberger accompanied me out to the front of the building insisting I might get lost in the maze of halls and rooms. I didn't protest since I was so grateful to him for telling me as much as he did, more than he should have, no doubt.

Taking a chance Pamela would be at work, I drove next to the law offices. She was there and seemed eager to talk to me. I had never been in her personal office, which was decorated in an odd combination of power images and feminine softness. Pamela's desk was big, modern, almost intimidating the way it dominated the room. Bundles of papers in great disarray were piled high on a side table, and cardboard file boxes were stacked like large building blocks on top of the file cabinet. Pamela sat in a huge, high-backed swivel chair behind the desk that looked like it might swallow her up. Yet the walls were pale blue and the drapes were boldly patterned in yellow roses with blue trim. Even the visitor's chair was upholstered in matching fabric with a ruffle around the seat. It was an unexpected touch of femininity that, unfortunately in this case, just didn't mesh.

I sat in the upholstered chair across the desk from Bernard's wife.

"I just came from the sheriff's office," I said, wondering if Pamela already knew about the additional charge of murder.

"So I guess you heard about it." Pamela's expression, calm till now, crumpled, and she pulled a tissue out of a drawer and wiped her eyes and blew her nose. "God, I didn't think it could get any worse, but it keeps on escalating."

"Who called you?"

"Bernard. A couple of hours ago."

"Did you tell him that you found the gun missing the night I was there?"

Pamela blew her nose again. “No, I didn’t volunteer it. If I told him, and they questioned him about it, he couldn’t lie to them. If the authorities knew I hadn’t reported it missing at the time, they’d just think I was making it up now to cover up for him. It puts me in a real bind. I should have thought of that the other night.”

“Well, hindsight is a great thing. But if you’d reported it that night, it might have made him a suspect in Raines’s killing even sooner since he was shot with a .22.”

Pamela crossed her arms on the desk and dejectedly laid her head on them for a couple of minutes. Finally, looking up she said, “No matter what I do, it seems I can’t help him.”

I felt sorry for her. I was sure Pamela was not used to feeling helpless.

“I’ve found out a few things,” I told her, “but no breakthroughs yet.”

Pamela visibly perked up. “Like what?”

“I’ve found out that Evan had been seeing a member of the Girl Scout staff fairly often. But according to her, he only used her as a sounding board to complain about Chris’s spending habits and her jealousy. This person says that Chris was driving them toward bankruptcy. On the other hand, when I talked to Chris, she insisted that Evan was the one who spent beyond their means. They both sounded sincere. And I've decided I'm a lousy judge of human nature as I haven't a clue as to who is telling the truth."

"Isn't it possible that Chris wanted to collect his insurance if they were in such dire straits? Or to exact revenge if she thought he was cheating on her?"

"It's possible," I answered, "but not probable. Surely Evan, as a bright young attorney whose earnings would keep increasing, would have been worth far more alive than dead. And I cannot picture Chris as insanely jealous and willing to kill over an affair."

Pamela studied me thoughtfully. "You have a hard time believing the worst about people, don't you?"

I could feel my face redden. I had no trouble at all thinking the worst of Pamela at one time. "Well, I suppose..."

"If you'd dealt with some of the people I have, you'd begin to question everybody's intentions."

"I hope I don't get to that point."

Now it was Pamela's turn to turn pink. She pushed her chair back and rocked slowly back and forth. "Yes, I guess I'm pretty down on human nature. Have you learned anything else?"

"Some creep in Evan's firm thinks Evan was involved in something illegal."

Pamela's face began to brighten. "Really? That might be a lead."

"He had no specifics so I didn't take him seriously. When I argued that Chris had very little money, he countered that Evan had probably stashed his illegal earnings offshore somewhere."

"That makes sense."

"I think it's the rambling of a jealous, mentally unstable man. He hated Evan's guts because he outshone him at the office. This guy's pathetic."

"Oh." The disappointment was strong in Pamela's voice.

"Well, that's it," I said. "That's all I know."

Pamela rose, unsmiling. I wondered if I was about to get fired from the case. I really didn't care at this point.

"Well, that's great," Pamela said, attempting to sound cheerful. "You're making progress." She extended her hand.

I rose too and shook her hand. "I'll keep in touch," I said.

EIGHTEEN

THAT EVENING LOGAN STAHL called. "How's it going?" he asked.

"So-so. I've gotten some juicy tidbits, but I'm not sure how accurate they are or that they'll help Bernard much."

"I was just listening to the local news." He was referring, of course, to the day's top story about Bernard being charged with Carter Raines's death.

"It's getting worse by the minute. Somebody very clever is setting him up."

"Tommi, I wouldn't be in your shoes for a million bucks. That's why I called. I finally got hold of Hank Wasserman at Midlothian."

"And?"

"He couldn't tell me much. Said Raines had stopped by the local office briefly to pick up some forms. He was in a hurry but spoke to Hank for a couple of minutes. They'd worked in the same office together in New York State some years ago. Then Hank transferred here, and Carter had eventually gone into investigations."

"And?" I wished he'd get to the point.

"Carter told him he'd found a paper trail he planned to follow. He alluded to the fact that it looked like some figures might have been altered on something but he wasn't sure where it would lead. He felt it worth looking into, though."

"Did he get any more specific than that? What did these figures relate to?"

"He has no idea. Carter rushed off for an appointment, and Hank never saw him again."

"Did he say who the appointment was with?"

"No. And Hank didn't ask."

"Well, thanks, Logan. I appreciate it."

I'd no more than hung up when the telephone rang again.

"Tommi, it's Frank."

How pleased I was to hear his voice. "I'm so glad you called."

"I just heard about Bernard. An old friend from Greensboro called me. It's unbelievable."

Frank Poag and Bernard are first cousins. His wife died of cancer over six years ago, and Frank, to get away from the haunting memories, moved to

Wisconsin. Not long after Bernard and I divorced, Frank's daughter, Nina, who's a friend of mine, was arrested for the murder of her husband. Frank and I were able to prove that she was innocent.

Had Frank lived close by, our relationship could well have developed into something significant. We talked occasionally by phone, and I thought of him more than occasionally, but there was too much distance between us, geographically if not emotionally.

"I'm still trying to take it all in," I replied.

"What kind of evidence do they have against him?"

I told him what I'd learned so far. "There's not much yet to vindicate him. I'm working on some leads, though."

"What do you mean? Why are you involved?"

"Pamela asked me to help out."

"Pamela!"

"That's right."

"Well, I guess I won't say what I'm thinking."

"You don't have to. I suppose I'm stupid to get dragged into this. But I know he didn't do it, so I couldn't turn her down."

"Look, I was thinking...I haven't seen you in about eight months. I've got some compensatory time coming to me. How about if I come down for a few days?"

I couldn't help smiling. He might say he was coming to see me, but I was sure it was more to help Bernard. There was a long period when the cousins refused to speak to one another. But after working together to exonerate Nina, the men resumed a relationship. The family ties were strong, and Frank was the kind of man who would feel obligated to help out whenever difficulties arose.

"Sure. Come on down, Frank." My casual encouragement belied my excitement at the prospect of seeing him. Though my feelings were mixed: would we be able to take up where we left off eight months ago?

"As a matter of fact my plane gets in at ten-thirty-five in the morning."

"Oh, great." I laughed. "What if I had said don't bother?"

"I'd have asked Nina to pick me up." Which proved it really was Bernard he was coming to see, damn it.

"Well, I shall see you in the a.m."

When I hung up, I hunted up Tee and fed him some catnip treats while I hummed a tune to myself.

THE NEXT MORNING I decided to call Annalee Turner before I left for the airport to pick up Frank. Perhaps she could give me an idea of where to hunt for "altered figures." She would at least know what Evan had been working on.

"It's Tommi Poag. I just need to ask a question or two," I said when I reached her.

"Okay."

"Was Evan involved in a particularly big case when he was killed? Something that would include handling a lot of money?"

"He was working on a couple of things. In fact, he was covered up with work. I was really surprised he took that Saturday off to be in that Girl Scout thing. Probably needed the break, though. He'd been here a lot of late nights."

"What were these cases?"

"Well, I can't give you confidential information."

"Just in general. What were they about?"

"One was a liability suit that involved big bucks. That's what he was most involved with. The other was a very big estate. Some multimillionaire had died. He'd asked Wes to help him out on that because he really didn't have the time for it."

"So Wes has been handling it?"

"He'd done most of the work on it, anyway, so he just kept on with it after Evan died."

"Thanks, Annalee."

So Wes and Evan had been working together. And it sounded as if Wes was doing most of the work while Evan probably got most of the credit, a circumstance that probably only fanned the sparks of jealousy that burned in Wes, anyway. And a situation that Wes might be able to use to undercut his nemesis. This certainly had some interesting possibilities.

FRANK'S PLANE WAS a few minutes early, and he was already picking up his baggage from the carousel when I arrived at the airport.

A slow "Frank smile," as I call it, lit up his face when he saw me. It's a smile so warm, so unaffected and genuine, that it always makes me feel it's there for me alone, that others are not privy to its special radiance, although I know that can't be true.

"You look great!" he said holding me at arms' length.

"You, too," I replied. I'd forgotten how green his eyes are or how appealing the laugh lines that crinkle up around his eyes and bracket his mouth, the only wrinkles in his squarish face. He isn't an especially handsome man, though his great smile gives him a certain dash, but he radiates good cheer.

I began to fill him in on the past week's events on the way to the Marriott. After Frank checked in, we went to Bistro 40 in the hotel for lunch where I continued to appraise him of everything I'd learned. "I think we need to check out Wes Cheloff, the guy in Evan's firm who tried to convince me Evan was doing something illegal or at least unethical. He was working on the settlement of a multimillion dollar estate with Evan, but Evan was so involved in a liability case that Wes was doing most of the work. I wouldn't put it past him to doctor papers purely out of spite, to make it look like Evan had his fingers in the till."

"How do you propose we approach this?"

"Well, his secretary wouldn't tell me a thing. Maybe Evan's widow, Chris, knows something about it. Surely he must have mentioned it to her. Let me give her a call and see if we can visit her."

When I reached Chris, she said she doubted she could tell us much about his work, but invited us to come and chat, anyway.

"Any little thing would help," I assured her.

The McCandless house was back to its normal immaculate state. I wondered how Chris kept busy once all the housework was done. Was she so compulsive she had to resort to tasks like scrubbing the grout in the shower with a toothbrush every day?

After introductions, I got right to the point. "Do you have any information on the cases Evan was working on? Did they give you any of his papers from the office?"

"Just his private papers. Anything to do with clients was passed on to other lawyers in the firm."

"Had he told you anything about a big estate that he was settling?"

Chris looked first at me and then at Frank, her forehead creased in concern. "What's this all about, anyway?"

I leaned over and patted her knee. "It's just a vague trail that could be worth following. But don't get your hopes up. I heard in a roundabout way that Carter Raines was looking into some kind of altered figures that might or might not be connected to Evan's death. Then Annalee told me that Evan and Wes were working together on an estate, but Evan was so tied up on a liability case that Wes was doing most of the work."

"What's that jerk done now?" Chris asked. This was what I had been afraid of, that Chris would jump way ahead to unsupported conclusions.

"Hold on," I warned. "I can guess what you're thinking, but we're a long way from knowing anything."

Frank had sat there quietly throughout the conversation. Now he spoke. "Did he give you a name or say anything about this estate?"

"Sure. I know the family because they belong to the country club. It was Irving Crossland. We weren't real close because they were so much older, but Evan had done other work for Irv and had played golf with him. I've been on some committees and things with his wife, Susanna. That's why he'd asked Evan to handle it. But when Irv died, Evan was so bogged down in the liability case that he'd asked Wes to help him. And then the little creep turns around and slanders him after he's gone!"

Frank and I exchanged looks but said nothing. Might as well allow Chris to let off some steam as long as she did it only to us.

"Look, Chris," I said, "could you do me a favor? Could you call Mrs. Crossland, tell her I'm looking into Evan's death, and ask her if we could speak to her about her husband's estate?"

"You'd better believe I will. And ask her to tell you anything you want to know."

I was getting nervous about Chris's state of mind. "It's really important that you don't give her any idea that there might be some mishandling of it. If you plant that idea in her head, she'll let her imagination go wild. You must keep what we've told you today in the strictest confidence. Otherwise you could jeopardize what we're trying to do."

Chris took a deep breath and let it out slowly. "I'll do anything you tell me to do if it will help to nail that little toady."

NINETEEN

THE CROSSLAND MANSION was only a few streets away from Chris's house, but it made the McCandless place look like a caretaker's cottage. One of the grandest homes in Greensboro, a rambling Venetian Renaissance brick palace featuring arcades and arches, Corinthian columns and a distinctive green-tile roof, it sat in the center of a huge lot that extended half a block. Built in the twenties, the home was surrounded by mature oaks, crepe myrtles, huge magnolia trees, and dozens of dogwoods and redbuds which made the extensive lawn seem more like a city park.

"What are you going to say to her?" Frank asked as we pulled into the driveway.

"I'm not sure. I'll have to play it by ear. Feel free to put in your two cents' worth."

Mrs. Crossland answered the door herself, no doubt waiting in the foyer for our arrival. She was a tiny woman whose face bore the stretched, unnatural mask of numerous surgeries. Her pinkish-yellow hair was thin but stylishly curled, and her casual slacks and blouse had the unmistakable lines of designer wear.

The minute I stepped into the dark, flag-stoned entrance hall, the strong odor of mildew almost overwhelmed me. As we were led into the "library," I could tell why: the furnishings, even the draperies, rugs, pillows and table runners must have been in the house since Day One. Everything had a distinctive twenties' look and the genteel shabbiness of eighty-year-old accouterments. The house had probably been built as most houses in the region were at that time with a dirt floor in the crawl space which allowed wetness to accumulate. Once that mildew permeated the walls and floors, it became a permanent adjunct to the building. And it didn't help that the windows were nearly covered by dark, heavy drapes that kept the rooms in a permanent state of gloom. I figured she was so used to the odor, she didn't even notice it.

Mrs. Crossland waved us into matching William Morris-style chairs covered in faded green-and-brown fabric. She sat down opposite us on an oak settee with tapestry cushions.

"How can I help you? Chris only told me you wanted to talk about Evan's managing of Irving's estate."

"Yes," I said. "I don't want to pry into any private matters, but I hoped you could tell me if Evan was handling it to your satisfaction."

"I wouldn't want this to get back to Chris," Mrs. Crossland fingered the elegant string of pearls that hung at her throat, "but it didn't seem to me that Evan was doing anything at all. It is always this Wesley somebody who keeps calling me about one thing or another."

"Has he called you often?"

"Yes, as a matter of fact. It seems he always needs to do research into this and that. I was sure Irving had everything in perfect order, but to hear Wesley tell it, everything's in chaos, and it's taking him many weeks to straighten it all out."

"Had you ever discussed this with Evan?" Frank asked.

"I was planning to. I'd made an appointment with him, but he was killed before we got together."

I noticed that her gnarled hands were shaking, and there was a catch in her voice.

"So what will you do now? Leave it in Wes's hands?" I asked, leaning forward to touch Suzanne

Crossland's arm gently to convey my sympathy and concern. I could tell she was emotionally fragile, and I didn't want to upset her further.

"I...I don't think so. I'm just not sure what to do, but I've been thinking about talking to Ralston Jeffress about it. Ralston's a senior partner, and I've known him for many years. We probably should have gone to him in the first place, but Irv was so impressed with young Evan. He wanted to help him along in his career. It's just that I hate so to make waves. I've always shied away from confrontation. But I can't let this go on much longer."

"Well, we won't take any more of your time. Thank you so much for your help, Mrs. Crossland. I hope you can get your problems straightened out." Both of us rose, Frank adding his appreciation, and we left the Crossland mansion.

"Whew," said Frank once they were back in the car, "do you suppose she's immune to that awful odor?"

"Must be," I answered, rolling down the window to let the fresh air flow over me, "I guess when you live with it constantly your sense of smell must atrophy or something. Anyway, what's your reaction?"

"Sounds like Wesley is having a field day with

the estate. Do you think Evan found out and was going to blow the whistle on him?"

"It's the most logical explanation yet for a motive. How about this for a scenario—Wes rips off Mrs. Crossland. Evan finds out. Wes kills Evan to keep him from reporting it. Now Wes is busy making it look like Evan was the one who was responsible so if it all comes to light, Evan gets the blame. A dead man can't defend himself."

"Exactly what I was thinking."

"But here's our problem. If the firm finds out what's been happening, they might just restore the funds and cover it up to save their reputation. We'd never be able to prove Wes had a reason to kill Evan. It seems to me that we've got to get our hands on the paperwork before it's altered, if in fact it hasn't been already."

Frank stroked his chin thoughtfully. "How could we possibly do that? I hate to be a pessimist, but I think our chance of getting the goods is about on par with winning the lottery."

"Come on, Frank, don't give up so easily. Look, why don't you come to my house and we'll hatch a plan. I'll even cook you some dinner since I owe you about nine times over. I have to warn you, though, my culinary skills have not improved since you were last here. You'll probably get a BLT or something equally gourmet."

Frank grinned. "I think I could deal with that."

We were silent as I drove to my condo. I thought again how very much I liked and admired Frank. Why did he have to live so far away?

I turned onto my street, and when I reached my building I saw that all the parking spots were taken. The main disadvantage of condo life as I see it is lack of adequate parking. When anyone has company, there simply aren't enough spaces to go around, and I end up having to find a place on the street. To make matters worse, that side of the street is a tow-in zone. I had to go down to the next intersection, make a U-turn and park on the opposite side. Luckily there were a couple of spaces open today. Often there was not.

I got out, locked my door and began to cross the street. Something moved in my peripheral vision, and I turned to see a tan older model car accelerate rapidly around the corner and head in my direction. Its huge chrome grill below the big round headlights resembled the demonic grin on the face of Satan. I knew it was aimed at me as surely as a flyswatter is wielded to annihilate a fly, but before I could react, something shoved me harshly from behind, and I went tumbling over the curb onto the tree lawn. I could feel the air disturbance as the car flew by narrowly missing me and heard a thud and a groan.

I had fallen headfirst, throwing out my arms to catch myself, and the thick grass cushioned my fall, but for a moment I lay there stunned, unable to move. As I turned to get up, I saw Frank lying in the street, his right leg twisted at an angle normally only rag dolls can achieve. Much more ominously, a rivulet of blood was running from the corner of his mouth.

Oh, dear Lord, I thought, *he's dead!* I stumbled over to him and knelt down beside him. His left arm was flung out onto the pavement and I felt his pulse. It wasn't strong but it was there.

A car stopped a few yards away. I felt momentary panic until I noticed it was blue, not the one that had almost run me down. A man got out and hurried to my side.

"What can I do?" he asked.

"Get help. Call the police and an ambulance."

He reached into his car for his cell phone and dialed 911.

Another car approached from the opposite direction and stopped in the middle of the street not far from us, emergency blinkers flashing. A young man got out, nattily dressed in a business suit. Without a word he approached Frank, took off his jacket and spread it over Frank's torso. "I'll go down to the next intersection and direct traffic so no one tries to come through here." He said.

A few people now gathered on either curb, but no one else offered to help. They merely stared with the vacant expressions of the terminally curious. I wanted to tell them to get lost, but it would do little good. I sat quietly beside Frank holding his outstretched hand, but tumultuous thoughts hurtled around my mind as I tried to make some sense of what happened.

Was it an accident? No, that car bore down on me as if I had some huge target painted on my body and it was aiming for the bull's-eye. I was supposed to be dead. Frank had seen what was happening and had pushed me to safety. *Please, God,* I prayed, *don't let him die because of me.*

Soon I heard a siren. It sounded to me more like a choir of angels singing the Alleluia Chorus than the piercing, godawful noise that ambulances normally make. An emergency vehicle pulled up and a young man and a woman hopped out and immediately began tending to Frank, taking his pulse, blood pressure, going over him inch by inch for injuries. The static monotone of the dispatcher's voice over their radio served as background music to their ministrations. I marveled at the calm, professional manner of these young people, relieved Frank was in good hands.

Soon two patrol cars arrived, one right behind the other, their revolving blue lights adding a ludicrous carnival-like atmosphere to the scene. One officer went to watch the paramedics work on Frank. The other approached me.

"Are you with him?"

"Yes, he's my friend. It was a hit-and-run."

"Can you describe the car?"

"It was one of those old, huge sedans, you know with all the chrome on the front. I don't know one car from another. But I'd guess it was a seventies' model."

"Color?"

"An ugly tan. Sort of khaki."

"How many in the car? And can you describe them?"

I shook my head forlornly. "I was out in the street and it was coming straight at me. I was in such shock I'm not sure if I even noticed. I think it was just one but I have no idea even whether it was a man or woman. Frank pushed me out of the way. Otherwise, I would have been hit."

"Did you see a license plate?"

"No, no...since we have only rear plates in this state. I was lying on my face in the grass by the time it went past."

"Okay, try to think back if you remember anything else. In the meantime I'm going to interview some of these bystanders."

I closed my eyes trying to see if my memory would come into any sharper focus. But all I could visualize was the grill of that car bearing down on me. I'd been mesmerized by it; I never looked up.

They were getting ready to load Frank into the ambulance now. He was hardly recognizable strapped to a backboard with formidable-looking bands, his head and neck braced by large blocks of foam, an inflatable splint on his leg, an oxygen mask over his nose and mouth, and a blood-pressure cuff on his arm. An IV solution hung above him dripping its contents into his other arm. I knew that it was not uncommon for accident victims to be transported this way only to be released from the hospital shortly afterward. But I didn't feel the least reassured.

TWENTY

I FOLLOWED THE AMBULANCE to Wesley Long Hospital. By the time I'd found a parking place, the paramedics had hustled Frank into an examination room in Emergency and the woman at the front desk demanded to know Frank's life history for the records. After I told her everything I knew, the woman asked me to remain in the waiting room until the doctors were through examining him.

"We'll call you, dear, when you can go see him," she said, smiling sweetly as if to deny the gravity of the situation. I wondered how people whose work brought them face-to-face with death every day coped with it. I didn't think I could. I sure couldn't be cheery about it.

After a short while I decided that sitting in the waiting room was like Chinese water torture: every agonizing minute that passed felt like another drop of water wearing me down, making me crazy. Several other people waited alone in forlorn silence while families huddled together, worry and strain showing on their faces as they spoke in hushed tones. Old, rumpled magazines were strewn about on tables but I couldn't concentrate enough to look at one. A wall-mounted TV set droned on with a game show, the ebullient contestants in stark contrast to the anxious occupants of the room. I knew I must call Nina, but I wanted to wait till I had something concrete to tell her.

I hadn't been there long when the policeman who had questioned me at the accident scene sat down next to me.

"Are you doing okay?" he asked kindly. He was a young man, rather short and stout, with friendly brown eyes. "I'm Officer Stern, by the way."

"I didn't hurt myself falling if that's what you mean. Otherwise I'm not so hot."

"That's understandable. Just a few more things I need to know. It won't take long."

I answered what questions I could about Frank, saying I'd notify his daughter Nina but couldn't help him much with anything pertaining to the accident.

"I still don't remember anything significant about the car or the driver," I told him. "But I had the distinct feeling he was deliberately trying to run me down."

Officer Stern looked surprised. "Why do you say that?"

I regretted I'd said it almost as soon as it was out of my mouth. Although I felt certain my investigation had precipitated the incident, I was reluctant to admit I'd been looking into Evan's death. The police were not likely to be overjoyed with my audacity in disregarding their conclusion that Bernard was guilty of killing both him and Raines. It wasn't that they could or would stop me from what I was doing, but they'd probably think I was looney tunes and would regard anything I told them with skepticism.

"It's just that he seemed to aim right at me. He never swerved or braked."

"He may have been drunk or he could have been looking elsewhere. I won't say you can't possibly be right, but most hit-and-run drivers are not homicidal maniacs," he said in a slightly condescending way as if he were explaining it to someone of limited intelligence. "They're boozed up or inattentive or maybe senile. And sometimes they're just plain scared so they don't stop. But hopefully we'll track him down and find out what was going on."

I felt my face redden. He did think I was overreacting. But I knew in my heart I was not.

It was nearly two hours before a doctor came into the waiting room and asked for me. He spoke to me quietly in the hallway.

"Mr. Poag has a broken left tibia and fibula, those are the two bones in the lower leg, a couple of broken ribs and a concussion. As yet he has not regained consciousness."

"Do you think he will soon?" This seemed ominous to me.

"We can't say. His condition is not life threatening, but it's impossible to tell in these cases. It could be hours, it could be days."

"Are you saying he's in a coma and he might not come out of it?"

"That's very unlikely, but not impossible."

I couldn't think of a reply. I was filled with remorse. It seemed as though I'd jinxed the life of everyone I knew and loved.

"We have an orthopedic surgeon on his way in to operate on his leg tonight," the doctor continued. "He might be in ICU for a day or so after surgery, but I shouldn't think any longer than that."

"What about the blood I saw running out of his mouth?"

"He cut his tongue. It took three stitches."

"Can I see him?"

"For just a minute."

He directed me back to a cubicle surrounded by curtains. "In there," he said.

Frank was stretched out on the examining table, an IV still dripping into his vein, a blood-pressure cuff on his arm like a mourning band. He was covered by a sheet and lightweight blanket even though it seemed warm in the room. He lay still as death.

I leaned over and kissed his forehead gently. "Didn't your mother ever teach you not to shove ladies around?" I whispered into his ear. I sat down in the chair beside the bed and watched his face, yearning for some fleeting sign of returning consciousness. But the only thing that moved was his chest rising and falling almost imperceptibly beneath the blanket. At least it meant he was alive.

A nurse began to push back the curtains. "Time to go to surgery."

"Take good care of him," I pleaded as I left.

I was directed to a pay phone down a corridor that connected the emergency room to the hospital proper. My cell phone was in the glove compartment of my car. Luckily, I had one of those small electronic address and phone number gizmos that

I kept in my purse. I dialed Nina's number, but all I got was her voice mail. The same with her cell phone.

I didn't want to leave such devastating news so I told Nina to get in touch with me as soon as possible, without saying why.

There was nothing more I could do here now. I'd check on Frank first thing in the morning.

It wasn't till I got in my car that the full impact of what had happened overcame me. My hands began to shake, and I could hardly get the key into the ignition. I hoped to God I could make it home.

TWENTY-ONE

IT WAS JUST AFTER midnight when the phone rang. I'd been in bed about half an hour but knew there was little hope of falling asleep. I'd lain there in the dark reliving the horrifying moment on the street over and over. I wanted desperately to expunge it from my thoughts, at least long enough to get some sleep, but it was like one of those tunes that occasionally sticks in my mind playing itself repeatedly until I want to scream.

"Tommi? Is something wrong?" It was Nina sounding frightened. "I hope I didn't wake you but you sounded so urgent."

"It's Frank, Nina. He was hit by a car this evening."

"Where is he? At home? There in Greensboro? Is he all right? Is he..." She paused and I knew she meant *is he dead?*

"He's still unconscious. He has a concussion.

And his leg is broken along with some ribs. He's at Wesley Long. He flew in this morning."

"I'll be there in thirty minutes." Nina lived in Oak Ridge, a small town northwest of Greensboro.

"Come to my house, Nina. They're not going to let us visit him in the middle of the night. They were taking him up to set his leg when I left. We'll call in when you get here."

When I hung up, I got up and put on blue jeans and T-shirt and made a pot of coffee. I didn't normally drink the real stuff after noon but I needed that shot of caffeine right now. While it perked, I sat in my rocker and held Tee on my lap, combing him as he'd never been combed before.

I hadn't seen Nina in quite a while as both of us had been busy. She and I had the shared bond of unfaithful husbands, but mine only dumped me, while she was accused of killing hers. Frank and I had managed to disprove that about eight months earlier.

It was nearly two when Nina arrived, looking exhausted and worried. She carried a small suitcase and a grocery bag with some milk, orange juice, a head of lettuce and some luncheon meat.

"What on earth?" I asked when she handed the bag to me.

"I just got back from the beach tonight. I had these left over and decided they'd go bad if I left them in my fridge. Have you heard anything more about Dad?"

"I called a few minutes ago. He was out of surgery and in the recovery room. Everything went okay with the leg."

Nina dropped onto the sofa like a rag doll. Tee, who hid from most visitors, jumped up on her lap, and she began stroking his back. I had long noticed how often people in stress did that. "What is Dad doing here, Tommi? I can't believe he'd plan a trip to the state without telling me. Or was it a spur of the moment thing? I've been at the beach for two weeks. I told him I was going, but I had no planned itinerary, just kind of drove around the Outer Banks and stayed where the spirit moved me."

"I was afraid you didn't know about the circumstances that brought him here. I tried several times to call you but never got an answer. After that, things got so complicated, and I got so involved."

Nina sat suddenly forward causing Tee to jump to the floor in alarm. "What are you talking about, Tommi?"

"Bernard was arrested for the murder of my

divorce attorney, Evan McCandless, and now they think he also killed an insurance investigator."

"What! I can't believe it! That is absurd."

Bernard had become close to Nina since she and her late husband, Cap, moved back to North Carolina from California.

I sat down beside Nina and gave her a hug. "Pamela asked if I would help look for anything that might exonerate him, and I told her I would. And it shouldn't surprise you to know that Bernard gave me a hard time. Finally said he'd go along with my involvement for Pamela's sake only."

Nina gave me a faint smile. "That sounds like him. Unbelievably stubborn. Tell me the whole story."

It took a while for me to cover everything that had happened since that terrible day a week ago when I found Evan shot in the head.

"So now what?" Nina asked when I'd finished.

"I have no choice but to go on. I'm convinced that car was deliberately trying to run me down. And why would anyone want to do that except to stop my prying?"

"You're putting yourself in a dangerous spot, Tommi."

"I can take care of myself." I spoke with more

confidence than I felt. “Your dad almost got killed over this. I’m going to find out who did it for his sake if for nothing else.”

“Do you think it was Wes in that car?”

“Oh, no. I think he’s too gutless to do something like that. He might hire someone to do it, though.”

“How can I help?”

I rubbed my chin thoughtfully for several minutes, staring at the floor. “I’ve been working on an idea while I waited for you to come. But I’m hesitant because I don’t want to put you in jeopardy.”

“If you’re willing to take a risk for Bernard after what he’s done to you, I certainly am. And especially now that Dad’s been hurt. The two musketeers, huh? Dad’s number three. If we’re one for all and all for one, we’d better get cracking, then. So tell me about this plot you’re hatching.”

“We’ve got to find out what Wes is up to. And the only way I can figure is to go to his office and look at his files.”

“Say what? Just coolly walk in and announce, ‘Wes, I know you wouldn’t mind letting me rummage around in your file cabinet?’”

“Not quite. That’s where you come in. Wes knows I’m his adversary. He’s going to have his guard up any time I’m around. By the way, have you sold your house yet?" Nina's home in Oak Ridge had been on the market since not long after her husband died. She decided it was way too large for one person. It had been too large for two, but Cap had loved to impress. It was so pricey, we both knew it would be hard to find a buyer.

Nina looked puzzled at the seeming incongruity of my question. "No, why?"

"I thought you might get an appointment with Wes under the guise of wanting him to handle the sale of the house. He won't know it hasn't sold. And my impression is that he doesn't specialize in any particular field, that he'll take whatever comes his way—divorce, wills, real estate, whatever."

"Okay. Then what?"

"Fifteen minutes or so into your appointment I'll call his office and say that his wife has been hurt in an accident and has been taken to the hospital. I'll disguise my voice."

"You mean he's got a wife?"

"Oh, yes, I checked that out. Poor thing. Never met her, but I can't imagine living with the jerk."

"So he rushes off to the hospital."

"You got it. And you look through his files."

"Don't you think he'd escort me out of the office when he leaves?"

"Tell him you need to use the ladies' room. Then sneak back in after he's left. I've been there, and since the john is just across the hall, you could easily do it without anyone seeing you."

"What would I be looking for? I can't very well carry files out of there."

"I've got this little digital camera you could put in your purse. That's one advantage of being a woman—you can carry almost anything in your bag without looking suspicious. I want you to photograph the Irving Crossland file, and Wes's appointment calendar for the past couple of weeks. I want to know where he was on the days Evan and Carter Raines were killed."

Nina sank back against sofa, laying her head against the folded afghan to stare at the ceiling. "I'll be honest. It scares the heck out of me. But I'll do it for Bernard and Dad. And for you. But don't we have to wait till Monday? What else can we do in the meantime?"

"I'm hoping we don't have to wait till then. My experience with lawyers is that most of them work on Saturday. And that's good because there would be no receptionists or secretaries around. Of course, they don't usually take appointments then. But if you tell him you're going out of town and can't easily get back to see him anytime soon, I'll bet anything he'd see you today. He strikes me as pretty desperate for work."

"That sounds like a plan."

"Come on, then. Let's try to get two or three hours of sleep. You don't want to look like a zombie when you go over there."

"I'll probably be quaking in my boots as it is. I don't need to shake from lack of sleep, too."

We went upstairs to our respective bedrooms. I was glad that Tee wanted to snuggle up beside me tonight.

TWENTY-TWO

NEITHER I NOR NINA slept well, and we were up by seven. Nina called the hospital and learned that the first ICU visiting hours were 10:00 to 10:30 a.m. Then she called her brothers and sister who were spread across the country except for a brother who lived out west. She'd wait and call him later when it wasn't the middle of the night. "No, don't try to come," she told them after describing what had happened to Frank, "there's nothing you can do. I'll keep you posted on his condition."

After that we sat silently reading the newspaper as we ate our cereal and drank our coffee. There was a small article in the second section about Frank being hit by a car, but few details were given.

"I'm anxious to see Bernard, too," Nina said. "I just want him to know I'm here to support him any way I can."

"I think he's home now. Pamela told me she was

finally able to get the bail money together. It was sky high, and it took some doing. My idea is this—we'll get the pictures of the documents developed at the one-hour service at the drugstore, and then we'll take them over to show Bernard. I'm sure neither of us could interpret the files, but he could probably tell whether there was hanky panky or not."

"But even if he did think something was wrong, he couldn't exactly tell the police what we did. And they'd know he wouldn't have access to those files."

"I'm hoping he or his lawyer might be able to convince other members of Wes's firm to check into it. If he could quote them some compelling evidence without telling them how he got it, they would probably want to follow up for their firm's sake if nothing else."

"You really think so?"

"Nina, to tell you the truth I'm grabbing at straws. I just don't know what else to do at this point. Got any better suggestions?"

Nina shrugged. "Nope, sure don't. Anyway, it's nine o'clock so I'd better call Wes."

As I had suspected, Wes was at work and willing to see Nina at eleven.

"I'll go visit Dad and then go on to the law firm

from there," she told me. "Should we drive two cars to the hospital?"

"Since they only allow one person in ICU at a time, I won't try to go this morning," I told her. "I'll see him later today. Do you have something to wear?" Nina had shown up the night before in jeans and an oversize sweater.

"I threw in a dress when I packed. I learned a long time ago to be prepared for any eventuality. My life with Cap was always so unpredictable."

When Nina was ready to leave she looked elegant in her mauve knit dress with a pale pink-and-teal scarf draped around her shoulders. But her eyes revealed her tenseness. "I hope Dad's better this morning. Tommi, what are we going to do if he doesn't come out of this coma?"

"He will, Nina. You know he will. It just might take a little time." I tried my best to sound confident. "And watch your step at Wes's. I'll call his office about eleven-twenty in case he's running a little behind."

I tried to keep busy after she left by making beds and doing dishes and the long-neglected dusting and sweeping. But my mind was on Nina every minute, wondering if she was finding Frank awake and improved over last night or discovering that he had worsened. I'd wanted to go to the hospital this morning, but I felt that Nina needed to spend the whole half hour with him this time.

At eleven-twenty sharp I dialed the number for Jeffress, Rigolosi and Latham. "May I speak to Mr. Wesley Cheloff please?" I asked the man who answered the phone.

"He's with a client. And his secretary is not in today."

"This is Officer Smith with the Greensboro police," I said in my most authoritative tone. "Mr. Cheloff's wife has been seriously injured in an accident and has been taken by ambulance to Wesley Long hospital." Wesley Long was the farthest from his office.

"Oh, god. I'll tell him right away."

The next hour was as bad or worse than waiting in the emergency room as I tried to imagine what was happening. Was Nina able to get back into Wes's office? Could she find what she was looking for? Was she able to take legible pictures? Would anyone catch her in the act? I chastised myself for putting Nina in such a position. If anything happened to her… It was too much to even contemplate.

It was twelve thirty-five when Nina came bursting through the front door, a wide grin on her face. "Piece of cake!" she proclaimed.

I could have danced with joy. For once, my plans had worked out right. "How's Frank?" I asked.

"They hope to move him into a regular bed by tomorrow. His vital signs are all good. But he's still unconscious. Though I thought he squeezed my hand a little."

"That sounds encouraging. Let's drop the flash card off to be developed and grab a bite to eat," I said.

"I'd like to stick my head in to see Dad again." Nina glanced at her watch. "The next visiting hours are at one."

I drove my Honda and we took the flash card to the one-hour processing lab at the drugstore and were at the hospital a few minutes after one.

I went in first. Frank lay peacefully on the bed as he had the night before, except that his leg was in a cast to his hip. A monitor near his head kept track of his heart beat, respiration, blood pressure and God knows what else; little blips and lines and bright changing numbers to indicate the life force that continued on without conscious effort on the part of the patient. But it had the effect of emphasizing how tenuous that life force can be.

I put my hand in his to see if he would squeeze it as he had Nina's, but there was no response that I could discern. Maybe Nina had imagined she'd felt it in her desire to see some positive sign.

I stayed only five minutes, allowing Nina to have most of the allotted time with her father. She had little to say when she came out but was much more subdued than she'd been when she came back from seeing Wes.

We grabbed a bite at a Wendy's and picked up the 8x10 pictures. I leafed quickly through the prints, mainly to make sure the records were legible. They were. Nina had done a good job. Then we headed to Bernard's house. I had called from the hospital to make sure he was home. He was on leave from the firm until the trial. They couldn't afford to have a possible murderer in their midst. Even legal firms have trouble when it comes to the basic presumption of innocence, particularly if it affects their bottom line.

Bernard came to the door as we pulled into the driveway. Nina jumped out of the passenger side and ran up to the house to embrace him. When I reached them, I shook hands with him solemnly, thinking all the while how ludicrous it seemed to be shaking hands with the man I'd been married to all those years.

"How's Frank?" he asked. I had filled him in about the events of the night before when I'd called, though I did not share my suspicion that it was no accident. He would have insisted I stop my investigation.

"He's stable, but not awake yet," Nina said, her lower lip trembling.

"I'm sure he's going to be all right. He's tough, Nina. Now what did you two want to talk to me about?" he asked as he led us to the family room. "You sounded rather mysterious over the phone, Tommi."

Nina and I sat down together on the couch while Bernard pulled up a side chair to be closer to us.

"You probably won't approve of what we did," I began. "But first let me tell you about Wesley Cheloff. Do you know him?"

"Cheloff? Didn't he help Evan out some during the divorce? I can't seem to get a mental picture, though."

"You'd remember if you saw him. Kind of fat and sloppy. Pretty unappealing guy."

Bernard nodded thoughtfully. "Right. I think I know who you mean. What about him?"

I described my visits with Wes and his ranting about Evan.

"See, I told you, didn't I?" Bernard assumed one of his self-satisfied looks. "And Cheloff wasn't the only one who loathed him."

"Are you referring to yourself, Bernard?" I knew that wasn't what he meant, but I couldn't resist the jibe.

"No, Tommi. Take a poll at a bar association meeting and see where he'd stand. He'd have come out dead last in a popularity contest." He suddenly seemed to realize he'd unintentionally made a grisly pun, so he took out a hankie and blew his nose with much ceremony, folding and unfolding the handkerchief carefully to cover his embarrassment.

"Be that as it may, can't we let him rest in peace?" I couldn't believe that Evan had been all that unpopular. Bernard was indulging in his usual tendency toward exaggeration. "What I'm trying to do is come up with a motive for his murder. So let me tell you about the Irving Crossland estate." I described the visit to Suzanne Crossland and her complaint about Wes's excessive involvement in settling the estate. Finally, I confessed to what Nina and I had done that morning.

Bernard said nothing for a moment, but his face

got that dark blotchy look that always preceded a heated argument. Since he usually chose to maintain a stony silence when he was mad, I knew this would be one of the rare occasions when he'd make his fury known vocally. "You stupid women! What are you thinking, anyway!"

Nina started to cry, but I wanted to slap his face. "We're thinking of your thankless hide, that's what!" I said softly, barely able to maintain enough self-control to keep from shouting back at him. "Have you come up with something better?"

Bernard got up and began pacing in front of the fireplace, his hand on his chin, staring at the floor. Finally, he came back and sat down. "Sorry," he said, looking at Nina but not me. "I don't want something to happen to either of you. Besides, what you did was illegal, and even if it shows anything, it can't be admitted as evidence."

"I know that," I said, feeling miffed. "I'm not that dumb. But I thought you could tell by looking through it whether it might point to motive. And if it did, you could get your lawyer to contact Jeffress, Rigolosi in hopes they'd look into it. After all, they wouldn't want their firm to look bad. If Wes is screwing up, they'd want to know about it.

And if they're aware that you know about it, they can't sweep it under the carpet."

Bernard sighed heavily. "All right. I'll look at the file, but I have many reservations about this."

Nina had recovered her poise by now. "You've always been willing to help me. Why shouldn't I try to help you?"

"Because you put yourself in a dangerous situation. What if something happened to you? My life is rotten enough right now without adding to it. If you got hurt on my account, I'd never forgive myself. Please don't make my life worse than it already is."

I marveled at Bernard's gift for making his concern for others sound purely selfish. I knew he was genuinely worried about Nina; but it came out sounding like he was primarily interested in himself. The poor guy needed to take a course on sensitivity.

But Nina apparently didn't interpret it that way. "I'm not brave enough to do anything really dangerous. What if he'd caught me in the act? If he's hiding something, he wouldn't want to call the police, would he?"

"If he is a murderer, Nina, he wouldn't hesitate to kill you as he killed Evan and Raines if he thought you were on to him. He couldn't do it there in his office, but he'd find a way."

Nina looked at him for a minute and then said, "Oh," in a chastened voice.

I had realized that what we did was risky, of course, but when Bernard put it so bluntly, I was more aware than ever that I might be getting in over my head, and even worse, I was pulling those I loved right in with me.

TWENTY-THREE

"OKAY," BERNARD SAID GRUDGINGLY. "Let me see those pictures you risked your necks for."

Nina handed him the envelope of pictures which he opened and glanced through quickly. "Hold on," he said laying them on the seat of his chair. He left the room and was back in a couple of minutes with a magnifying glass. "This should do it," he said.

We sat quietly while Bernard studied the file. Nina seemed lost in her inner thoughts while I inspected my nails, noticing how badly I'd neglected them of late. But it didn't seem like the time or place to bring out my nail file. My shoes needed polishing, too.

After about thirty minutes, Bernard put the pictures back in their envelope, and stuck the magnifying glass into the crack between the cushion and the arm of his chair. "I don't think you're on the right track," he said. "There's no doubt Cheloff has probably padded his time here. There's so much emphasis on billable hours in law firms. As you well know, Tommi, lawyers must bill a set number of hours each month or off with their heads. If he's as unlikeable as you say, he may have trouble getting enough work to fill his quota. But I don't think Mrs. Crossland's complaints are well-founded. She doesn't realize how much work is involved in an estate of this size even if everything seems to be in good shape."

"Are you saying he's on the up-and-up?" I asked, frustrated. "Why is he saying all these things about Evan then? I was sure it was to hide his own wrongdoing."

"I'm more inclined to think he merely took advantage of Evan's death to vent all his pent-up hatred of him, something he couldn't do when Evan was alive. And remember, he might very well believe that Evan was involved in something crooked. I, too, share the view that it was perfectly possible."

"Maybe we should have gotten other files. There are probably other cases where he's ripping off the client, and Evan found out," I said, disappointed and surprised that Bernard was not ready to jump immediately to the conclusion that Wes was guilty.

Especially when his own neck was on the line. "I'm just not ready to let him off the hook."

"Hold on," said Nina, holding up her index finger. She delved into her handbag, sorting through its contents till she brought out a small spiral notebook. "I used all the space in the camera photographing the file, so I copied from Wes's appointment calendar for the past two weeks." She handed it to Bernard.

"Look here," he said, reading from it. "Friday, Saturday and Sunday, May 18 through 20. Wasn't that when Evan was killed?"

"Yes, Saturday morning, the 19th," I said.

"According to his calendar, he attended a seminar in Kansas City. Jason Fredericks from our firm went to that. Let me give him a call and see if he can confirm that Wes was there."

He left the room. I rubbed my temples; I was getting a splitting headache.

"One great idea—down the tubes," Nina said to no one in particular.

Bernard was back within five minutes. "Jason says Cheloff was definitely there. He was so annoying, he stood out like a sore thumb."

"Darn," I said.

"Double darn," Nina added.

“When was Raines killed?” Bernard asked.

“Tuesday the 22nd,” I told him. “Early in the morning.”

Bernard flipped over several pages. “He attended a morning kaffee klatsch with the Jaycees. Started at seven. Doesn’t seem likely he would have time to kill someone first. Do you want me to check and make sure he was there, too?”

“If you want,” I answered, subdued. “But I suppose it’s a waste of time. So no sense in my wasting more time on Wesley. If I’d thought about it, he’d never have the nerve to kill anyone. He’s nothing more than a windbag.” I stood up to leave.

Bernard arose, too. He handed the spiral notebook back to Nina. “I know you mean well, but stay out of trouble, will you? I realize Pamela asked you to help, Tommi, but why don’t you let my investigator handle it. It makes me nervous to have you two wandering around chasing flimsy leads.”

I nodded a perfunctory goodby and hurried to my car, slamming the door so hard when I got in, Nina jumped perceptibly as she came down the front walk. When Nina got in beside me, she put her hand on my shoulder. “He doesn’t mean to be so hurtful. He’s just worried about us.”

I bared my teeth and growled like an angry dog.

"Jeez, that man makes me crazy. No matter how hard he tries to say the right thing, it always comes out wrong. I should quit this no-pay, thankless, frustrating job of trying to save his neck."

"You may not want to do it for Bernard, but what about Dad?" Nina pleaded.

I chewed on my lip for a minute. "You're right. If it weren't for Frank pushing me out of the way of that car, I'd be dead. I'll do anything to find out who was responsible for hurting him."

IT WAS NEARLY FOUR when we arrived back at my house. Nina wanted to see Frank again during the four o'clock visiting hours. Bernard had said he planned to visit him later in the evening. I told her not to be alarmed if I wasn't home when she got back. "I've got to check out other possibilities," I said.

I didn't know where to turn next but Raines's alleged words, "altered records" wouldn't leave my mind. What other records were there? Chris said that all of Evan's client files were still at the office, but she had several boxes of personal papers. Could there be something in them? I might as well at least look.

Chris, as usual, was at home when I called. I

wondered why she didn't find something outside of the house to occupy her, get her mind off Evan's death. But it was probably too soon. I decided I should recommend a grief support group to her. I'd heard they could help a great deal in the mourning process.

"I don't mean to keep bugging you, but I'd like to see you again," I told Chris when I called.

"You don't bug me. I long for company."

Chris seemed subdued when I arrived at her home. She was gracious as ever, but it seemed to be taking a lot of effort. All the indignation she'd shown against Wesley was gone, replaced by a melancholy that was all-pervasive. Even her movements, usually brisk and energetic, were now slow and lethargic. Grief, in its insidious way, was making inroads.

"How was your meeting with Suzanne Crossland?" she asked. Apparently she'd missed the small article in the paper about Frank. I hated to add any more bad news to what she already was dealing with, but I told Chris about the hit-and-run driver. "Frank saved my life by pushing me out of his way."

Chris reacted with stunned silence, tears coursing down her cheeks.

"That's why I'm determined to get to the bottom of this. I think whoever killed Evan is responsible."

"Wesley?"

I sighed deeply and shook my head. "Apparently not. He has a substantiated alibi."

"Who then?"

"That's what I've got to find out. Didn't you say that some boxes of Evan's papers were sent from his office?"

"That's right. But only personal papers. Nothing connected to his work."

"Have you read through them?"

Chris looked down at her hands, fingers touching together like a child making a church steeple. "No, I haven't. I've been afraid I might come across something I'd rather not see." She looked up for a minute, her eyes full of distress, then looked down again. "I was afraid I'd find out about an affair. And I just don't want to know about it if there was one. I'd rather go on thinking that he was faithful."

I could not reassure her, much as I wanted to. "I understand, Chris. But would you mind if I looked through them?"

"Whatever for?"

"I'm not sure. Just thought there might be something that would trigger an idea, give me some direction."

"The boxes are in the basement. Do you want to take them home so you can look at them more comfortably?"

"That would be great."

Chris took me down to the basement where three cardboard cartons were stacked in a far corner, covered by a sheet. Out of sight, out of mind. It took two trips to carry them up and put them in the back of my car.

"Do me a favor," Chris said as I prepared to leave. "If you find out he had a lover, don't tell me about it. In fact, I'd just as soon you would destroy the evidence. Then I can go through the papers some day without worrying about what I'm going to see."

Poor Chris. Determined to cling to a squeaky clean memory of Evan. One thing for sure: it was easier for a widow to do that than a divorcee. The widow can have a very selective memory, choosing those things she wishes to recall. But a divorcee has a living, breathing ex around to refute any fantasies she might harbor about their life together.

I was exhausted by the time I'd hauled all three boxes into my condo. The darn things weighed a ton, and my back hadn't fared too well this past week, anyway. Between being pushed out of the speeding car's way to sitting in hospital chairs more suited to a torture chamber, I'd endured more than my sacroiliac could handle with grace.

I stacked the boxes on the floor next to the kitchen counter that divided living and eating areas. Lifting the first one onto the counter I began to go through the contents. There was a lot of gibberish that I merely scanned: notes, memos, clippings. There were no client files, of course. It was mostly a hodgepodge of outdated personal items, scribbled budgets, notes probably taken while talking to a stockbroker, even a shopping list or two, all the accumulated detritus that clutters everyone's life.

Just then the front door flew open, and Nina staggered in under the load of two huge grocery bags.

"I noticed there wasn't much in your fridge so thought I could get some stuff for dinner."

"There's rarely much in my fridge. I usually pick up a frozen dinner on the way home from work if I don't get carryout somewhere."

Nina set the bags down on the portion of the counter that wasn't covered with stacks of papers.

"There's some more in the car. You wouldn't mind if I cooked supper would you?"

"Mind? Would I mind if I won the Publishers Clearinghouse sweepstakes? Dear, you just said two of the most glorious words in the English language, 'I'll cook.' Music to my ears."

Nina laughed and went out to get the rest of the groceries. Since I had cluttered up the place where we would eat, I cleared away Evan's papers till after supper.

Nina described her visit with Frank while she prepared a stir-fry dinner of chicken and Chinese vegetables. "He seems about the same," she said, her voice betraying a diminution of optimism over his condition. "They're still not sure when they'll transfer him out of ICU."

I didn't try to be artificially cheerful this time. I just couldn't keep on pretending Frank was going to wake up any minute. "I know he's getting excellent care there," was all I could manage.

While we ate, I explained about the boxes. Nina was always so circumspect about not prying that she hadn't even asked what the boxes were, apparently believing they were my personal papers.

"Haven't found anything interesting yet, but I'm

hardly halfway through the first box. Chances are I'll find zip, though."

After we did the dishes, I lifted the box I'd been working on back up on the counter. Nina sat beside me, gazing absentmindedly at the papers while I checked each of them. Her mind was probably at the hospital with Frank.

About three-fourths of the way through the box I found a small date book. Mostly it was business appointments, but under February 17 was the entry "Barb—O.Henry Hotel." Barb was listed twice in March. So, it did appear that something was going on between them. Would they meet at a hotel to discuss Chris's spending habits as Barb had claimed? Not hardly.

I set the date book aside. It would not go back into the box for Chris to discover.

But I had to get to the bottom of this. Barb wasn't going to lie to me the next time around. I knew it was useless to call her tonight since it was Saturday. Barb always talked about their active social life which seemed to include most of the parties that were written up in the society column. I also knew they didn't attend church. They typically "recuperated" from all that fellowship on Sunday morning. So I hoped I could reach her first thing tomorrow.

I went through the rest of the box but found nothing of any interest. After being up most of the night before, my vision was beginning to blur and my back ached and I decided to call it quits. Nina, who had sat beside me in some kind of half trance, seemed relieved when I closed up the box and put it away. We both read for a very short while and then gratefully fell into our respective beds. But I slept fitfully again for most of the night.

TWENTY-FOUR

I COULD HAVE SWORN I hadn't slept at all, but I woke with Tee standing over me on the bed poking me with his nose as he was wont to do each morning about six-thirty. I didn't need an alarm clock with him around, even though it was annoying on weekends and holidays. It made no difference that his food bowl was usually half-full. I always had to add a handful of his favorite dry food before I could convince him he wouldn't go hungry.

I put on my robe and fetched the Sunday paper to read with my breakfast of bagel, juice and coffee. After I'd rinsed my dishes and put them in the dishwasher, I considered going through Evan's boxes some more, but decided to watch Sunday Morning on TV instead. Even investigators need some time off now and then. Besides, I needed to call Barb before I went any further. I knew Barb always slept late on Sundays, and it wouldn't help to wake her up and have her in a foul mood when I asked my questions. And frankly, I was sick and tired of the whole mess. If anything, I was going backward. Right now it seemed that Barb was the only one who might point me in a new direction, and it was a lead I didn't even want to pursue. I liked Barb, in spite of the fact she'd been involved with Evan. She'd been the best camp director the Girl Scouts ever had, and Evan's death had made her position that much more difficult. I wondered if parents were still withdrawing their children from Camp Galimore.

Nina came downstairs just after I had turned the TV on low so as not to wake her. She was already dressed in gray slacks, white blouse and Guatemalan-fabric vest. "Going over to see Dad," she explained.

I felt guilty about missing visiting hours again, but Frank's condition depressed me greatly. Since it was Sunday maybe I should pray over my Sin of Avoidance. "I've got to make an important phone call," I told Nina as though that excused me. But I did want to talk to Barb in private.

By ten-fifteen I realized I'd better make the call before Nina got back since I'd used it as an excuse to stay home. I was grateful when Barb, not her husband, answered the phone. "Hi, Barb. It's Tommi. Could we discuss something personal over the phone or would you rather meet me somewhere?"

There was a short silence while Barb absorbed the significance of this. "Are you asking if I'm alone?"

"Or out of hearing range."

"I am. What's going on?"

"I have Evan's date book here. I'm looking at February 17 and March 1 and 5."

Silence.

"Are you there?" I was afraid she'd dropped the phone and left.

"What is this, anyway, the Inquisition?" Barb asked sharply.

"I had trouble believing what you said about Chris, that she was spending all their money."

"Okay, so I made that up. I didn't want my husband to find out."

"I wasn't going to tell your husband—or anybody else."

"How could I be sure of that? Actually we were together only twice. The third time was to tell him I didn't want to see him anymore. But he kept calling me and begging to see me again."

"So it wasn't true about knowing each other for years."

"Oh, yes, that was true. To tell you the truth, he confessed he liked me in high school, but never let on. For some reason, when he found out I worked for the Girl Scouts, it was like he had a high-school crush all over again. I was the one who asked him to be on the Board, not realizing that I was unleashing an infatuation that went back years. I was curious and flattered at first, but I realized shortly that I wasn't all that interested. And I didn't want to jeopardize my marriage."

"Did it ever occur to you that your husband might have found out about it?"

"Shaun? I'm sure he didn't have a clue. For one thing Evan and I met during Shaun's office hours. Dentists can't just take off at any time so there was no chance of accidentally bumping into him."

"Maybe someone else found out and told him. Maybe he was insanely jealous and decided to kill Evan."

Barb laughed, a low melodious laugh, entirely inappropriate to the conversation. "I guess you've never met Shaun. He wouldn't hurt a mosquito. He's the most benign person on this earth, which is why he's in therapy, because he hates to hurt people when he drills on their teeth. Wrong profession for him but too lucrative to give up. Anyway, he has Saturday hours. The only pain he was inflicting that Saturday was on someone's molar. Call his office if you want to double check."

"I'll take your word for it. Sorry to have to ask you personal questions, Barb."

"That's okay, Tommi, just as long as you keep all this to yourself."

"Of course I will. How are things at the office?"

"Better. Parents are registering their kids for camp again now that someone's in jail for the shooting. I know that doesn't make you feel too great."

"Just wonder how they'd feel if they knew it was the wrong person." I decided not to mention that Bernard was out on bail.

"You're still convinced of that?"

"More than ever."

When I hung up, I kicked the wastebasket nearby, knocking it over and sending its contents flying onto the floor. Luckily there was nothing but paper in it, and I contemplated the scattered pages as I tried to reconstruct my shattered image of Evan. I knew now that my version of Evan was distorted—the fun house mirror again. Perhaps it was the timing. Evan had come into my life at my lowest point, and he had done much to rebuild my tattered ego. Yes, I was beginning to understand now that he shamelessly flattered all women, making them feel attractive and clever. It was just his way. But even if he was not always sincere, it had helped me immensely during one of my most troubled times. From then on, I saw in Evan my own manufactured version of the man, refusing to accept that he was an incorrigible flirt, and that his charming personality was consciously tailored to propel him to the professional heights he coveted. I wondered now if I would ever be able to discover or understand the real Evan. Or if there even was a "real" Evan.

TWENTY-FIVE

I HAD JUST CLEANED UP the spilled contents of the wastebasket when Nina called. "They're taking Dad to surgery shortly," she said, her voice fearful. "The pressure inside his skull has increased, and they need to relieve it."

"I'll be right there."

I hadn't dressed yet, so I hurriedly pulled on slacks and sweater and drove to Wesley Long Hospital. I parked the car and sought out the surgical waiting room where Nina said she'd meet me. The room was slightly cheerier and brighter than the emergency room had been, but its occupants looked every bit as distressed. Nina sat slumped in a chair, chewing on a fingernail. She didn't notice me till I sat down beside her.

"What happened?" I asked.

"There's some sort of medicine they put in the IV to reduce the swelling of the brain, but it didn't seem to be working. So they have to relieve the pressure surgically." She grabbed my hand with both of hers and squeezed till it hurt. All I could do was squeeze back. Maybe now was the time for prayer. Instead of praying half in jest for my Sin of Avoidance, I prayed with all the sincerity, if not experience, I could command. I hoped God would forgive me for being a novice at this, but never before had I felt such a need.

The hours crept by at an agonizing pace. Others were summoned by the doctors and left the room to see their loved ones or go home. Nina worked a crossword puzzle she found in a discarded paper, but I couldn't concentrate enough to help her. I wondered if it was raining yet because it looked dark and threatening as I drove to the hospital. Yet in this interior, windowless room, the fluorescent glow shone twenty-four hours a day, no matter what the world outside was doing.

It was nearly three hours before a young man, dressed in surgical greens, came into the room. "Poag?" he asked. *Good heavens,* I thought, *he looks like he's barely out of high school. How could he be a brain surgeon?*

Both of us jumped up, and he walked over to us

in a weary sort of gait. “I’m Dr. Rubin,” he said, his dark eyes and somber face not giving us a clue.

“Is he okay?” asked Nina.

“We relieved the pressure. His vitals are good now. But we can’t say for sure that there isn’t some brain damage. We’ll just have to wait and see.”

I wondered how long they would keep saying that: “Wait and see. Wait and see.” Was that all they could come up with? I felt a rush of resentment that the medical community with all its miracle machines and cures couldn’t come up with something better than that.

“Can we see him?” Nina asked.

Dr. Rubin looked at his watch. “The next visiting hours in ICU are at four o’clock. Why don’t you come back then?”

I took hold of Nina’s arm. “Let’s go home and grab a bite to eat. We can come back later.”

We walked dejectedly to the parking lot. It had rained while we were inside, but now there was only a light sprinkle. The sky still looked threatening, though, a murky, dismal ceiling hovering over us that felt oppressive and unstable. My car was at one end of the lot and Nina’s at the other. “Here,” I said, working a key off of my key ring, “Let me give you my extra house key. I’m going by the drugstore to pick up a prescription I called in. I'm having trouble with allergies. Anyway, it appears you're going to be around for a while, so you should have one." We hugged briefly for moral support before getting in our respective cars.

The drugstore was just a few blocks from my condo. It was nearly empty, the weather no doubt keeping people home, and my prescription was ready for me. I didn't chat with the pharmacist as I usually did. I was too depressed for one thing, and I wanted to get home before it started raining hard again. I pulled out of the parking lot and drove down Lawndale Drive as lightning flared ahead of me. Two blocks from the pharmacy Lawndale intersected with Lake Jeannette Road. Half a block away, I saw the light change to yellow. I applied my brakes, but my foot went to the floor. The car didn't slow down in the least. A stab of panic that felt almost like a seizure gripped me. The light turned red, and cars that had been stopped on Lake Jeannette Road began to move. I downshifted with a grinding of gears, but it only slowed the car slightly; it had too much momentum at this point. Frantically I laid on the horn, but the cars were already in front of me. They had nowhere to go. I couldn't steer left, a car was in the lane beside me. To the right, a group of people stood waiting to cross the street. At least my horn seemed to have alerted them. Two stepped off the curb, turned to gape at me and hopped back up on the sidewalk. I had to go straight ahead. Gripping the steering wheel ferociously, I hung on. If I only had an air bag. But I couldn't afford a new car.

Just as I reached the intersection a huge old blue Plymouth, its body festooned with patches of red rust, came from the right. An elderly black man was driving it, and he stared at me in startled amazement just before I hit his right rear fender. The clash of metal tearing into metal replaced my blaring horn with one of the most sickening and fearsome sounds in my experience. The Plymouth swung around counter clockwise at the impact, and my Honda hurtled on across the now-empty street into a mailbox on the opposite corner. I saw it crack and give way before me as my car ran up the post a short way before coming to a convulsed stop.

An eerie silence enveloped me. The world seemed to have stopped in its tracks. Then a ringing began in my ears and I could feel my heart bounding in my chest. Taking a limb by limb assessment of my body, I found that everything seemed to work, my arms, legs, fingers and toes. I felt sore across my front where the seat belt had dug into me as my body was thrown against it on the sudden impact. And now my knee was starting to throb where it had apparently collided with the steering column. But I didn't seem seriously hurt.

"Are you okay?" A middle-aged man had approached my side of the car, and was attempting to open the door. It made terrible metallic protesting sounds as he pulled at it, but it eventually swung partially open.

I was afraid to move, sure that I'd discover some terrible injury I wasn't aware of. But I unbuckled the seat belt and gingerly climbed out of the car.

"Careful, now," the man said, holding out his hand to help me. The front end of the car was elevated a couple of feet off the ground as it rested on the bent-over mailbox post, and I had to hop down to the pavement.

My poor, dear car. The front end was mangled beyond belief. Engine parts were indistinguishable from body parts in an abstract sculpture of twisted and crumpled steel. But there was little damage from the front door post on back. Maybe my prayers back in the waiting room had had a side effect. Somebody was sure watching over me.

I looked around me. Crowds were now congregating on the street corners. Cars were stopped in all directions. Two more men were approaching me. The other car was smack in the middle of the intersection, but turned almost 180 degrees. The rear fender that I'd hit was torn and bent in against the tire that was now flat. But I was relieved the driver seemed to be okay. He was standing looking at the damage to his car, chin in hand, shaking his head in disbelief.

I assured the two men who came to check on me that I was all right, but in truth my knees were so shaky I needed to sit down. I hitched myself back up on the car seat to wait for the police to come. Either I was having incredibly bad luck these days, or someone truly was out to get me. I heard the sirens shortly and wondered if it would be the same officer who came when Frank was hit less than two days earlier. What would he think? Would he believe me this time?

But the policeman who arrived was unfamiliar. I was just as glad.

"Do you want me to call EMS?" he asked me.

"No, I'm okay. Just shook up."

"License and registration, please."

He checked those out, verified my address and

gave them back. Then he copied down my insurance information. "Can you tell me what happened?"

"My brakes failed. The pedal went clear to the floor."

The officer wrote it down. "I see your car was inspected recently."

"Yes, just last month."

"We'll check the brakes when we have it towed to our lot."

I sat back down in the car while he talked to the other driver. Finally, a flatbed tow truck for my mangled Honda and a regular tow truck for the Plymouth arrived to cart both cars away, mine to the police yard and his to be fixed.

Before the other driver left, I went over to speak to him. Even though my insurance company advised never to discuss an accident or admit guilt, I couldn't let it go.

"So sorry it happened. My brakes wouldn't work."

The man's rheumy eyes twinkled a little. "I just come from church. The good Lord musta heard my prayers."

"Mine, too." I said. "Hope they can fix your car okay."

"Ain't all that bad. Just needs poundin' out and a new tire." Apparently he was used to such incidents.

A crash of thunder startled us both, and it began to rain huge drops that spattered on the ground the size of half dollars. The policeman who'd been sitting in his patrol car writing up a report on the accident came over to us. "Can I take you both home?"

"Naw, thanks. I's gonna call my son," the man said. He pulled a cell phone out of his pocket and draped his raincoat over his head as he walked to the shelter of a large tree.

"I'd appreciate it very much," I told patrolman. I sat with him in the car as he finished up the report.

"Paperwork," he grumbled. "We drown in it." The rain was coming down hard now. Finally, he finished, gave me my copy with all the insurance information on the other driver, and drove me the five blocks home.

I ran into the house holding my purse over my head, but my hair was plastered against my face, my sweater clung to me damply and my feet were soaked. I kicked off my shoes inside the front door, and wiped my wet face with a Kleenex from my purse.

Nina was sitting at the counter drinking a cup of coffee when I came bursting in. "Oh, I didn't realize it was raining so hard," she said at my bedraggled appearance.

"That's the least of it," I said, pulling my damp

sweater away from me and trying to shake it dry. “This hasn’t been my day—or weekend for that matter.” And I told her about the accident.

“Your brakes wouldn’t work? Gosh, Tommi, had they been checked lately? What do you think happened?”

“I think the brake line had been cut.”

Nina looked at me in horror. “You’re serious?”

I walked into the kitchen and poured myself a cup of coffee and sat down on the dining stool beside Nina. “Can you believe that all the things that have happened are a coincidence? That car the other night was aimed at me, not Frank. Today was their second try. I don’t want the third time to be the charm.”

“Oh, Tommi, what are we going to do?”

I shrugged. “Be damned careful, and find out who’s doing it.” I looked at my watch. “We don’t have much time before visiting hours with Frank. Let me make myself a sandwich and then we can go. After we leave the hospital, if you’ll take me out to the airport, I’ll rent a car. I can’t contact my insurance agent till tomorrow.”

“As long as I’m here, we can use mine,” Nina said.

“I don’t want to put you out.”

“You won’t put me out. For one thing, I plan to go everywhere with you. I don’t think you should be alone.”

“Oh, come on, Nina. That’s not necessary.”

“It is necessary. And I’m going to be stubborn about this.”

I said nothing but went into the kitchen to make myself a turkey, cream cheese and cucumber sandwich. I didn’t want to admit it, but I was glad Nina had been insistent.

TWENTY-SIX

FRANK SEEMED ABOUT the same. The main difference was the helmet of white bandages that enveloped his head. He lay still, unaware of our presence as always, but at least the lines and numbers on the monitor seemed to be rhythmic and stable. Even though only one visitor was allowed at a time, the nurse, who winked and smiled in conspiracy with us, allowed Nina and me to go in together. She looked about forty, was chunky, prematurely gray and had one of the sweetest faces I'd ever seen. Her name tag said Angela Fernandez. I thought that was appropriate because she did indeed seem like an angel to us. We sat quietly by Frank's bed for the whole thirty minutes, each engrossed in our own thoughts.

The rain was still a steady downpour when we came out of the hospital, and I was nervous the whole way home, as I had been on the trip over. I'd never liked being in the passenger seat, anyway, I wanted to be driving and in control, but now I was overcome with anxiety every time a car coming in our direction wavered slightly or if a vehicle in front of us turned or stopped without warning. My foot involuntarily hit an imaginary brake about once every block, and I gripped the sides of my seat in dread. If Nina was aware of this, she never let on. Actually she was a pretty good driver. But I would have been a basket case riding with anyone.

We returned to my house and Nina busied herself making spaghetti for supper. If the circumstances had been different, I would have delighted in the luxury of not having to cook, but there was no joy in anything right now. A veil of gloom had descended over my life, precluding any feelings of contentment and cheer.

The phone rang and I answered it.

"Mrs. Poag?"

"Yes."

"This is Detective Farrell of the Criminal Investigation Division. We found the car that hit Frank Poag."

"You did? Whose is it?" Maybe this was the break that I needed. A tiny surge of hope gripped me.

"It was a stolen vehicle. Taken from a used car

lot down in Archdale the day he was hit and abandoned on a dirt road in Randolph County." Archdale is about twenty miles southwest of Greensboro and Randolph County bordered our Guilford County to the south.

"Do you know who was driving it?"

"No ma'm. Couldn't get any decent prints. Way we know it was the right car, we found some fibers on the grill that matched Mr. Poag's clothing. The right headlight was broken out, and the glass at the scene matches the glass in the remaining headlight."

"What now?"

"Well, we'll keep the case open, of course. Our best hope is that we hear something through an informant. Sometimes these guys get cocky and brag about their misdeeds."

"And if that doesn't happen?"

"Well, ma'm...we'll just keep on doing the best we can." He sounded about as positive as the quarterback of a last place team.

"Thanks for calling." I felt like kicking the wastebasket over again, but I didn't want Nina to know I could be so childish. Instead I calmly repeated what I'd been told, not realizing till I'd finished that I'd torn the paper napkin beside my plate into a pile of itty bitty pieces.

"They'll never find him," I said dejectedly, "let alone ever believe that it was deliberate."

"What do you think they'll say if they find your brake line has been cut?" Nina was stirring her homemade spaghetti sauce in the big Dutch oven, steam rising from it like a witches' brew.

"They'll probably say it was an accident. Something sharp was laying in the street, and when I ran over it, it just flew up and cut the line."

"Heavens, you are cynical."

"I guess. But I don't think they tend to take us seriously. You know, hysterical women etc., etc. I think it's probably improved some on things like spouse abuse and rape. But something like this—it just seems too much like the figment of an overactive imagination."

"We'll just have to prove them wrong then," Nina said as she drained the spaghetti and served up the plates.

"Mmm, delicious." My mouth was full so I pointed at my plate. I swallowed and said, "Guess I'll go through those other two boxes tonight. Not much else I can do at this point."

Once the counter had been cleared, I hoisted another box onto it and began to look through it piece by piece. I wondered at times why Evan had kept all this stuff. Ninety percent of it seemed totally worthless; it should have been relegated to the trash can long ago. I hadn't realized he was such a string saver.

I was almost halfway through the third box when I found a file folder that said "cookie sale—duplicate records" on the tab. Inside, Evan had a page for every cookie chairman in the council. Each chairman oversaw a number of troops and collected cookie money from each of them. At the top of the page was the name of the cookie chairman and how many boxes of cookies were ordered, broken down by troop. He then recorded the proceeds as they came in.

I knew that there were big bucks in cookie sales, but I'd never realized just how much. Thousands of dollars were involved. I'd once been told that cookie sales amounted to about sixty percent of the council's income, but I had no idea how large their budget was.

I went through the file looking for names I recognized. I saw Yvonne Geisinger's name, a woman I'd worked with years ago. I was surprised Yvonne still had a troop. Then I came to a page with Melanie Tyler's name at the top. Her district had one of the largest orders in the council, but very little money had been turned in. On paper clipped to the page was a terse note: "Give Melanie till May 21 to remit proceeds."

Give Melanie until May 21 to turn in money or what? I wondered. Had Evan threatened her with something? Why hadn't she done it? It seemed that most of the other money had been turned over to him some weeks earlier.

It was a quarter till ten, but I knew Chris always stayed up for the late news so I dialed her number.

"Me again," I said when Chris answered. "Quick question. What happened about the Girl Scout cookie sale? Had Evan finished it up or was it still going on?"

"It was winding down, but I know he still had some work to do on it."

"So did the staff take it on?"

"No, Melanie Tyler felt she could handle whatever was left to be done. So she volunteered her services. She was already a cookie chairman, anyway."

"What did she do for records? I found some in these boxes."

"Really? Those must be copies. Melanie asked if I had any of the records and I told her no, but to talk to his secretary. Annalee then gave her the file which she found on top of his desk."

"What day was this, Chris?"

"The Monday after Evan died. Melanie apologized fervently for having to intrude, but said it was important to have those records right away. Something about having to get a report into national."

"Okay, that's all I needed to know. Thanks, Chris."

Nina was listening to this with undisguised curiosity. "What's the scoop?"

"Something very strange." I told her what I'd found and what Chris said.

"So what do you make of it?"

"I don't know. I'm not sure. But I think I need to talk to Melanie. Not tonight, though. I want to talk to her in person. When Ty isn't there. Let's go to bed. I'm feeling sorer by the minute. I'll bet I'm covered with bruises by morning."

"Go soak in a hot bath, why don't you."

"Great suggestion. I believe I will."

TWENTY-SEVEN

SURE ENOUGH, when I woke the next morning, I ached all over, but especially just below my left knee where a nasty bruise in shades of pink and blue had blossomed overnight. Marks on my shoulder and diagonally across my chest had appeared, as well, where I'd slammed into the shoulder harness. Those bruises I didn't mind so much. The alternative was something I didn't want to think about.

Nina was eating breakfast when I got downstairs. She'd even fed Tee.

"You're an early riser," I said.

"Didn't sleep too well. Seemed better to get up than to go over and over things in my head while lying there."

"If I can make an appointment to see Melanie this morning, could we drive over there after visiting Frank?"

"Sure."

I fixed myself some breakfast and at nine dialed Melanie's number.

"Hey, Melanie," I said when the young woman answered the phone, "It's Tommi. How are you?" My voice sounded so falsely cheerful I hoped Melanie didn't catch the forced lightheartedness of it. I assumed she knew nothing of the events of the past couple of days and would not question my good spirits.

"Fine. You know how it is with kids. Same old, same old."

"I've been thinking of you. Thought you might like some adult company. And I have a friend visiting that I'd like you to meet. But I don't want to bother you if Ty is off duty." I didn't want to give any indication that I had a serious matter to discuss. I wanted instead to witness Melanie's immediate reaction to my questions without the influence of her husband's presence.

"He's working day shift now doing undercover work. Come on over."

"It'll be about ten forty-five before we can get there."

ANGELA WASN'T ON DUTY when we got to the hospital so we had to take turns visiting Frank. I was so distressed at seeing him unchanged I wanted to shake him by the shoulders and pull him upright in bed. I had the overwhelming urge to yell, "Snap out of it! Open your eyes and talk to me!" Instead I laid my head on the side of his bed and cried torrents of tears, all the ones I'd held back these past few days. When they finally stopped, I felt drained, but it was cathartic, too. I wiped my eyes and hoped they weren't too red when I joined Nina in the waiting room.

After we left the hospital, I directed Nina to Melanie's house. I was beginning to wonder if the confrontation I'd planned would produce anything helpful. Maybe there was a simple explanation why the money hadn't come in. But Carter's words "altered records" kept going through my mind. Was he referring to the cookie records? It seemed so ludicrous somehow—Girl Scout cookies. But there was a lot of money involved.

Melanie greeted us with such apparently genuine pleasure, I found it hard to believe she could be involved in any wrongdoing. Yet I had learned time and again that things were often not what they seemed. I introduced Nina, and Melanie invited us in.

Brian and Annie were playing in the living room.

Brian ignored me and continued to play with a toy auto, but Annie came over and raised her arms to me. It broke my heart, considering what I was about to do, but I picked her up, gave her a kiss and a hug, and put her back down.

We all sat down in the hastily straightened living room, and Melanie, ever the gracious hostess, offered refreshments. "How about coffee and Girl Scout cookies?" she asked.

Nina and I both declined, but it seemed like the perfect opening.

"I've been going through some of Evan's papers," I said, "ones that were given to Chris."

"Really? Why is that?" Melanie asked innocently. "Are you looking for something that might incriminate her? I've really wondered about her with that insurance policy and all."

"No, I don't think Chris had anything to do with it."

"Oh," Melanie couldn't seem to think of anything else to say.

"I did find duplicate records of the cookie sale, though."

Melanie looked startled for a minute until she visibly pulled herself together. "I didn't realize he'd made copies," she said breezily. "I volunteered to take over the sale for the council. We were close to wrapping it up, anyway."

"According to his records, you hadn't turned in over seven thousand dollars from your district. There was a note saying he was giving you till May 21st to get it in."

Melanie's face reddened noticeably. "I had trouble collecting from some of the troop leaders. There are always a few who drag their feet on turning in the money."

"You're saying it's all in now?" I fixed my gaze unswervingly on her, daring her to lie.

"Oh, sure." Melanie pushed her hair back from her forehead and brushed invisible lint from her dark slacks. "I turned in the records already."

"Suppose I advise the Executive Director to do an audit on the campaign. I'll suggest that all of the troop leaders in your district be contacted about the amount of money they earned and how that compares to the numbers on your report."

Melanie put her face in her hands and said nothing. Brian had picked up a block and began to bang it on the edge of the coffee table, inflicting dents on the edge of the fake mahogany top.

"Stop it, Brian!" Melanie shouted, grabbing the block from him, which sent him into howls of rage.

I waited a couple of minutes till his cries settled down to a subdued sobbing. "What should I do about this, Melanie?"

Melanie began to cry now along with Brian. It was a duet of sobbing.

"Let me take the children into the kitchen for some cookies," Nina said, seeing that their mother's tears upset them. She reached for Brian's hand, but he pulled away and clung to his mother's legs. Annie, however, consented to go to with her.

Finally, Melanie gained control and picked up Brian and soothed him. As he laid his head against her breast, she began to talk, all the while staring down at him and stroking his head. "Ty's addicted to gambling. He likes to bet on the pro basketball teams, and he ran up a big debt. The guys he owed threatened us, and Ty was desperate. He told me I had to give him some of the cookie money." She chewed on her lip for a moment before going on. "He was sure he could win enough to pay the cookie fund back, but he had worse luck than ever, and there was no way he could do it. He said I had to change the records so it would look like all the money was in." She finally looked up at me again and spoke barely above a whisper. "So that's what I did."

I couldn't understand how someone could risk his job, his family and his future in order to bet. Especially a policeman who'd vowed to uphold the law. But that was the nature of the sickness, like any addiction, I knew.

We sat in silence for a few minutes. Brian had quieted down, and Nina and Annie were having their "treat" in the kitchen.

"Okay, now, here is the $64,000 question, Melanie. Tell me what happened at Camp Galimore." I didn't know if Evan's death was connected to all this, but in Melanie's emotional state, if she knew anything at all, now was the time to prime the pump.

Melanie broke into uncontrollable crying. She put Brian down on the floor and hugged herself in despair as her body heaved with anguished sobs. Brian, thankfully, seemed engrossed with a toy truck. He was too young to comprehend the enormity of his mother's grief.

Finally, she gained some control again and said in a tiny voice, "Ty made me do it."

"Do what, Melanie?"

"He made me send Evan over to the field."

"But I thought he went to relieve himself." This was the part I could never figure out.

"No." She blew her nose noisily. "I told Evan I thought I heard someone scream over in that direction. I told him a couple of rough-looking men had been seen hanging out near camp. That wasn't true, of course, but it was enough to get him to investigate."

"Why would you do that, Melanie? Why would you participate in a killing?"

Melanie laid her head back against the couch, drained of all emotion. She flung her arms out to her sides in a gesture of helplessness. "I didn't know he was going to kill him. Ty said he wanted to scare him, intimidate him, in hopes he would give us more time. I finally had to confess to Evan why the money was missing, and he had threatened to go to Ty's superiors if I didn't turn it in. Ty knew he would lose his job, probably go to jail. His whole life would go down the tubes."

"Why didn't you tell the sheriff or police when you found out what had happened?"

"Because I'd been involved. I've got three kids and no money and don't know where I'd go or what I'd do if Ty went to jail. And I could go to jail, too. Then what happens to my children?"

I understood what a desperate position she was in.

"I had no idea what he planned to do. As far as I

knew, he was going to scare Evan into giving him more time, and he promised me he would be able to get the money. I thought everything was going to be all right at last. I can't believe how naive I was."

"Melanie, as far as I'm concerned you're as much a victim as Evan and Carter."

Melanie looked at me with listless eyes and said nothing.

"To kill two people for seven thousand dollars," I mused. "I'm assuming he killed Carter, too."

Melanie nodded mutely.

"Ty thought Raines was getting too close to the truth?" I asked.

Melanie visibly struggled with her emotions. She spoke quietly in a flat voice. "Raines must have had a chance to look through the cookie sale file on Evan's desk when he went to talk to Annalee. He would have seen Evan's notes. I didn't get over there to pick up the file till later. He called and made an appointment to talk to me Tuesday morning about the cookie sale, so we had a pretty good idea that he'd guessed what was happening. Of course, Ty killed him before he could meet with me."

"Why frame Bernard? He hadn't done anything to Ty."

"Ty thought they'd call Evan's death an accident and close the case. But when Carter started snooping around, Ty decided he'd have to get rid of him, too, and make it look like Bernard was responsible for both killings. He'd heard about the malpractice suit Evan had filed against him. When you're around the courthouse a lot you learn about these things. And he knew there'd been bad blood between them since your divorce, Tommi. He thought it would make a good motive."

"But how could he know that Bernard couldn't verify his whereabouts both of those mornings?" I asked.

"Because he'd driven past Bernard's office on the way out to camp and noticed his car parked there. You know he has that vanity plate that says 'B. T. Poag.' And it was the only car in the lot, so he knew he was alone. He decided then and there he could fall back on framing Bernard if things started to come apart. When Raines started poking around, it seemed like the perfect solution. So when he arranged to meet Raines, he called Bernard and gave a false name to set up an early morning meeting, figuring it was so early no one else would be at the law office."

"Surely Bernard would have recognized his voice," I said.

"He's good at disguising it, something he learned when he was active in dramatics in high school."

I got up and went over to sit beside Melanie. I was torn between feeling extreme pity for her and thinking that somehow or other she could have extricated herself from this mess. But I knew she had to consider her children first and foremost.

"Look, Melanie, go with me to the police department," I urged her.

"Oh, I…I can't. What will Ty do? I've been so afraid since all this has happened." She was genuinely terrified.

"Once you tell them everything, he'll be put in jail and won't be able to hurt you. We'll stay with you and do whatever we can to help."

Melanie pondered my request for several minutes. Finally, she said, "Let me call a neighbor to look after Kelly when she gets home from school"

Kelly, the second-grade Brownie, was as winsome as the other two children. I wondered what would become of them all. How terrible that these precious children would undoubtedly suffer as a result of their father's actions.

TWENTY-EIGHT

MELANIE EXPLAINED TO ANNIE that we were going for a ride. That brought a smile to the face of the little girl who had come back to the living room with Nina once the decision was made. "Can we go see Daddy?" she asked. I almost broke down at that.

"Not now, honey," her mother said, "but we are going to the police station."

Brian was much calmer now, too. Nina led them out to her BMW, and Nina and I got in front while Melanie and the children climbed into the back.

We were only half a block away when I recognized Ty driving an unmarked car toward us. Nina, of course, didn't know him, so she drove blithely on, but I felt ill with dread. Maybe he wouldn't notice his wife and children in the backseat, I thought, knowing how unlikely that would be.

"Hey, where are you going?" he called out his open window as we passed each other. "I decided to come home for lunch." His car came to a halt in the middle of the street.

My heart began to race. What should we do? Stop or run for it? But Melanie told Nina to stop, and Ty backed up till he was opposite us. Melanie calmly rolled down the rear window to talk to him. "We're going to Wal-Mart for diapers. I ran out of them and these ladies offered to take me," she said. "We'll be back in a few minutes. You can make your own sandwich." She rolled the window back up.

Talk about grace under pressure. I couldn't believe it was the same woman who had been an emotional basket case only a few minutes earlier. But then she'd proved what a great little actress she was over the past days.

Nina picked up speed again and continued down the street. I looked behind me and saw Ty pull into his driveway, then back out again and follow us.

"He's behind us," I said. "We're going to have to go on to the store and pray that he leaves after that."

I told Nina to turn left at the next corner, and we drove up Battleground Avenue. We pulled up in front of Wal-Mart, and everyone piled out of the car and went inside. Out of the corner of my eye, I saw Ty park in the next row.

Once inside, I used my cell phone to call a cab company and gave instructions to be picked up at the opposite end of the store at the garden center entrance. “It’s an emergency,” I told them. “I need one as soon as possible.”

“He should be there in less than ten minutes,” the dispatcher said.

Then I told the others to head down to the garden department while I hung out at Customer Service, which gave me a clear view out the front door.

After a few minutes I saw Ty get out of the car and saunter toward the front entrance. I ran to the opposite end of the store where the others waited by the garden hoses and pesticides.

I hurried them out the door, but the cab had not yet arrived. The five of us huddled behind the row of riding mowers, the adults watching nervously for the taxi. I kept looking back at the door, expecting Ty to come charging out at any moment. Although the store was large, it wouldn’t take him long to realize we’d left. Brian, in his mother’s arms, was getting whiny, and Annie was pulling on my hand saying “Donalds, Donalds.”

“She wants a hamburger,” Melanie explained.

Just then a bright yellow cab came down the drive to where we waited and drove up beside us.

We scrambled in hurriedly, and just as I closed the door, I saw Ty come out of the door behind us.

"What's going on here?" he shouted, and started running toward us. "Stop!"

"Let's get out of here," I said to the driver. "Floor it, mister!" Thankfully Ty look disheveled in his undercover disguise, or the driver would probably have heeded his command.

As the cab sped away, I watched Ty run back toward the other end of the parking lot. I knew he was heading for his car.

I ordered the cab driver to take a roundabout route to the police department, figuring Ty by now had realized where we were headed. Though it would take us a little longer, my real concern was that Ty would catch up to us and force us to stop. He had a gun, and he could easily take us hostage and drive us God knew where. By taking the indirect way, we managed to elude him.

NINA AND I SAT IN Latoya's living room around six that evening. Ty was not yet in custody, and I felt it would be unsafe to remain at home till he was apprehended. I'd planned to go directly to a motel until this ordeal was over, but when Nina and I had stopped by my condo to pick up some clothes, making sure he was nowhere in sight, there'd been a message on my answering machine from Latoya. "I haven't heard from you in a while," she'd said. "What's going on with your investigation, anyway?" So I called her to invite her to have dinner with us.

Latoya had insisted that she cook for us instead. So we headed for her apartment on Market Street.

"Before we eat, you have to tell me what's going on."

"Blackmail, huh?" I laughed.

"Of course. You like to live dangerously it seems."

So I told her all that had happened since Wednesday.

"How awful," she said when she heard about Frank. "How is he?"

"Unchanged this morning," Nina told her. "We haven't been able to get back there since."

"What kept you so busy?"

Latoya's eyes grew wide in disbelief as I told her of Melanie's confession. "Where is she now?" she asked.

"In jail while bail is being arranged," I said. "Until they catch Ty, she's safer there. The wife of my boss offered to keep her children till their grandparents could pick them up. I knew it would be unsafe to keep them at my place."

"Did Melanie know how Ty got hold of Bernard's pistol?"

"When he took the rifle over to hide in Bernard's garage, he thought there was a good chance Bernard would have some kind of weapon in the house. So he picked a lock and searched until he found the gun in the night stand. All this with gloves on, of course."

"And how did he manage to meet up with Raines?"

"According to Melanie, he called him anonymously, said he wanted to give him information that would help his case, and arranged to meet him."

"Don't you suppose Carter would think it strange that he wanted to meet behind a building?"

"Ty told him he wanted money for his information, so it was natural to do it in a secluded place."

"So then he shot him and tossed the gun in the trash."

"Not quite so casually. He paid the homeless man to 'find' the pistol in the dumpster and turn it in to the police."

"What a devious mind." Latoya fingered her loop earrings as she contemplated Ty's Machiavellian schemes. "Do you know if he was involved in running down Frank and in your car crash?"

"The police feel sure he hired someone the night Frank was hit. And Ty could have been responsible for my accident since my car's always parked out front. As all of this came out this afternoon, the cops called the lot where my car had been towed. They checked the brakes and found the line had been cut. Just as I thought."

Latoya leaned back, closed her eyes and rubbed her forehead. "It just seems so incredible. I like Melanie a lot. I'd never have believed all this of her. Or Ty, either. Cookie money. Of all things to steal."

"He needed it desperately, and it was there," I said.

"I think Melanie needs support and understanding more than anything," Nina chimed in. "She was in a terrible position. If she turned him in, she knew she'd be prosecuted, too, and she had her kids to think about. And most of all she was terrified of Ty."

"She sure put on a good front. Remember the potluck supper the night before the Disaster Day exercise?" Latoya said to me. "They seemed happy then."

"She'd learned how to fake it," I said. "She

wanted everyone to think what a happy family they were. But I agree with Nina that she deserves our support."

"No question," Latoya said.

Then she hopped up. "If you're going to the hospital, I'd better get to work in the kitchen. Why don't you guys see what's on the news."

We had no more turned on the local news when the anchor announced Ty's arrest. He'd been found in Archdale, staying at the home of the man he'd hired to run me down. The man had an arrest record going back many years.

I called to Latoya, "Did you hear the news? They caught Ty. I guess I can go home after all."

"What a relief! I guess that about wraps up all the loose ends now," Latoya said.

"No!" Nina exclaimed. "It doesn't. Not until Frank is well."

After dinner Nina and I drove in silence to Wesley Long Hospital. It had been an emotionally exhausting day, and we were both deep inside our own thoughts.

I was glad to see that Angela was on duty. When she saw us, her face lit up with her beatific smile.

She came out from behind the desk and gave each of them a welcoming hug. “Guess what?” she said. “Frank’s awake and asking for you.”

TWENTY-NINE

FRANK MADE A QUICK recovery after regaining consciousness, and there seemed to be no permanent damage. He was discharged from the hospital by the end of the week, and Nina took him home with her to recuperate from the broken leg. I visited him often the next four weeks till he was able to return home to Wisconsin. I hated to see him go, and he acted as though he hated to leave me. Was our relationship forever destined to be a long-distance one?

Ty and Melanie were tried separately in the fall. There was some call for moving the trials out of town because of the pretrial publicity, but in the end they were held in Greensboro. Ty was tried first and given two life sentences, one for Evan and one for Carter.

Melanie had been out on $50,000 bail. No one seemed to know who had posted the bond since her parents couldn't afford to, and Melanie had no assets in her name. The jury deliberated for two days, and in the end she was convicted of being an accessory after the fact and given probation because of the extenuating circumstances. I was enormously relieved at the outcome.

After the verdict was announced, Bernard, who had also been attending the trial, came up to me. "How about a cup of coffee?"

We went to Krispy Kreme and ordered coffee and doughnuts. This was the first time I'd talked to him since shortly after Ty's arrest. At that time he and Pamela had come to my home to thank me for my help. They both heaped gratitude and praise upon me until I'd blushed with embarrassment. But it was great to have Pamela falling all over me. What a high!

"Have you heard from Frank lately?" Bernard asked as he poured way too much cream in his coffee.

"Yes, I talk to him fairly frequently on the phone. He's doing great. Leg's as good as new. No after effects from the concussion. He's been back to work for some time."

"He's very fortunate. And how's Chris? Haven't heard a thing about her in a long time."

"She's doing okay. Sold her house and bought

a condo in the same complex I'm in. She invested the insurance money and is even taking a course in interior design. I think she'll do well at it."

"It's good she's keeping busy. I imagine this has been a tough time for her. She couldn't put it to rest until the trials were over."

"That's true. But I know she'll work hard now to get on with her life. She'll always have to live with the sorrow that her husband was murdered, but I think she'll be okay."

"I hope so."

"Well," I said, "I'm so glad Melanie got probation. Her kids need her. She's a good mom. By the way, she says she doesn't know who posted bond for her. Do you happen to know? I'm curious."

Bernard toyed with his doughnut, pulling off little pieces to nibble on. "I did. Or rather Pamela and I did. We thought she needed to be out of jail so she could care for her children. Besides, she never should have been charged in the first place. The D.A. wanted to make Brownie points."

"If that's what he's after, let him sell Girl Scout cookies," I quipped.

"You know, Tommi," Bernard went on, "I'm not so proud of everything I've done over the past few years. I guess I look on helping Melanie as partial atonement for my actions."

"I'm speechless, Bernard."

"You don't have to say anything. Just try to look upon me a little more kindly than you have in the past. That's all I want."

I nodded my head slowly at him. "I believe I can manage that."

* * * * *